# Nate was *only* a client

Still, Emma's fingers twitched at the memory of that night. She'd spent half the party resisting until finally she gave in to temptation. He pressed a kiss to her fingers.

"You taste of truffles," he'd murmured.

Had he detected the throbbing of her pulse or the racing of her heart in response to his closeness? "What else do you sense?"

"You could drive a man wild."

Tingles like faint electrical impulses had swept through her body, and she'd pressed closer to him. His long, lean body was the shape she found most attractive in a man, with wide shoulders, narrow hips, a long neck and strong jawline faintly shaded by stubble.

The memory elicited a shiver of desire she couldn't blame on anything but attraction— the way that stubble had felt so enticing when she kissed him.

But she'd resolved never to willingly cross his path again. So what on earth was she doing now, walking up to his front door?

Dear Reader,

Welcome to my first book for Harlequin Superromance, after a long spell writing traditional romances and romantic suspense for other Harlequin lines. I've always enjoyed reading Harlequin Superromance books because they explore not only a page-turning romance between a capable, modern woman and an equally strong, modern man, but we also meet their friends, family and their world. This makes the writing so much fun.

I particularly enjoyed researching the recipes Emma Jarrett—a chef—cooks for heart surgeon Nathan Hale. For some of the dishes, I reached back into childhood to the foods my mother cooked, reminding me of home, comfort and security. It's good to see that some of the foods, like homemade sausages and meat loaf, are being reinvented in contemporary versions. It seems the more worrying daily life gets, the more comfort we seek in traditional foods—and romance. In this book I try to provide a generous helping of both.

The Bay Walk around a beautiful section of Sydney Harbour is also one I've done. If I have to work off my indulgences, why shouldn't my characters? *Bon appétit.*

Valerie Parv

# With a Little Help
## *Valerie Parv*

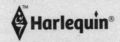

TORONTO NEW YORK LONDON
AMSTERDAM PARIS SYDNEY HAMBURG
STOCKHOLM ATHENS TOKYO MILAN MADRID
PRAGUE WARSAW BUDAPEST AUCKLAND

Recycling programs
for this product may
not exist in your area.

ISBN-13: 978-0-373-71697-5

WITH A LITTLE HELP

**Printed in U.S.A.**

## ABOUT THE AUTHOR

Valerie Parv always wanted to be a writer, penning her first novel in an exercise book at the age of eight. That novel resides in the State Library of New South Wales, among their collection of her papers. She's tried her hand at many things including owning and running a coffee shop where her double chocolate fudge brownies were a big hit, but says nothing beats the sheer joy of cooking up a new romantic story.

For my cheering section,
the bats, with whom brainstorming
is way too much fun; for Leigh who also made
brownies and talked catering with me;
and for CH always.

## CHAPTER ONE

To EMMA JARRETT, FINDING her mother waiting in her office meant only one thing—trouble. Cherie Kenner-Jarrett didn't venture out of the eastern suburbs of Sydney without good reason, although her reasons were seldom good for Emma.

Ignoring her mother's tiny frown, she slid her patchwork velvet backpack off her shoulders and parked it on the desk.

"What happened to the Miu Miu bag I gave you for your birthday?" her mother asked. Cherie's own bag was Prada as usual, Emma noted. Her charcoal suit over a frilled pink shirt had the distinctive cut of an Aloys Gada, her mother's favorite designer.

Cherie's hair was styled in a flawless chin-length bob with a sleek, off-center part highlighting her sea-green eyes. Emma's hair was a lighter reddish-gold, like the last embers of sunset, but flared out in an undisciplined cloud—the reason she usually wore it twisted up and imprisoned in a bear-claw clip. A couple of extra inches in height made her look slimmer than her mother, although Cherie actually weighed a little less, watching her diet with a resolve Emma couldn't match while working in the food business.

Since her mother sat behind the desk, Emma took the visitor's chair, a recycled wooden kitchen chair she'd painted citrus to match the billowing folds of curtain disguising the window's small size and view of the brick wall next door. "Your bag is too—special—for every day. This backpack is one of my own designs. The material came from a vintage velvet skirt I found at the markets. Aren't the colors amazing?"

"Amazing," Cherie agreed without conviction. "It's good that you keep up with your hobby. But if it means you sold my gift online, I don't want to know." Her manicured hand swept across a sheet of paper in front of her. "I see the bank's concerned about the business exceeding your overdraft limit. Why didn't you come to me or your father?"

No point protesting about her mother's right to read the letter, Emma knew. As a teenager growing up in Bellevue Hill, she'd never had the pleasure of opening her own mail. The letters had been neatly slit before reaching her. "In case there was something we needed to know about," was the excuse. Emails and instant messages fared little better until Emma learned to password protect them. Then there'd been lectures about the dangers of the internet and parental need to keep their child safe. "Your father and I worry about you," her mother had explained. "In our work we see the harm that unsupervised internet activities cause families all the time."

Emma's parents were in practice together. A pediatrician, Cherie was marginally more successful than her obstetrician husband because of her high profile in the media. Issues like child protection were her specialty, and she was a frequent guest on talk shows.

At first Emma had been proud of her mother's fame, until she realized she and her brother provided the case studies for many of Cherie's theories. To the media, Cherie made much of being a mother herself, when in truth, their housekeeper spent more time parenting Emma and Todd than their parents did. Running a demanding medical practice plus writing and public speaking meant family interactions generally came down to "quality time," not Emma's favorite term.

"Most businesses struggle in their first few months," Emma said, suppressing the urge to sigh. She wasn't prepared to ask for financial help from her parents, knowing she would lose some of her independence. Being the only civilian, as Todd called her, in three generations of medical practitioners was tough enough. Becoming a chef and opening a catering business had really put her beyond the pale. She wasn't giving her mother any more reason to find fault. "Thanks, but I'm doing okay, Ma."

"You know I don't like being called 'Ma.'"

"You don't object when Todd does it."

"Yes, well."

Cherie didn't have to add that anything Emma's older brother did was fine with her. Unlike Emma, Todd was establishing himself as an endocrinologist, to his parents' delight. So she masked her surprise when her mother said, "This visit is about what I can do for you."

"You need my catering services?" she asked warily.

Cherie looked uneasy. "Not me, Nathan Hale, the heart surgeon. His thirty-fifth birthday party's in three weeks and he's been made head of his department, both causes for celebration. I'm sure you remember Nate. It's only been nine weeks since you met at our office Christmas party. The two of you spent enough time together, before you left in his car."

Emma felt her face start to heat and looked down before her mother noticed. "The name rings a bell." Mostly alarm bells. Of any night, that was the one she most wanted to forget. She'd never come on to anyone the way she had with Nate Hale.

Now her mother was proposing Emma have him as a client. Good grief. If he was only now turning thirty-five and already head of a department, he must have inhaled his medical studies with his mother's milk.

She lifted her hands palms upward. She could

hardly tell Cherie the real reason she didn't want to work with Nate, so she used the only other excuse she had. "Renovation on the kitchen hasn't even started, Ma. There's barely room for Sophie and me to work together, much less the people I want to hire. It's too soon for us to take on a large project."

As usual, her mother demolished Emma's objections with a gesture. "You can do anything you set your mind to. Besides, your father and I have already recommended your service to Nate."

Emma felt herself start to drown. "Why?"

"You keep telling us how well you're doing." Cherie tapped a finger against the bank's letter. "Even if this suggests not all is going smoothly."

"Love This Catering is doing fine." Emma dragged in a calming breath. "Exceeding the overdraft was a small oversight. Things will improve once I get the kitchen upgraded and my team in place."

"How will you stay afloat until then if you reject every decent job that comes your way?"

The same way we've managed for the past five months, she thought. On a wing and a prayer. But she couldn't tell her mother that. Instead she said, "Doing work Sophie and I can manage with the facilities we have, and the monthly chef's dinners we hold here. The mailing list for them is growing all the time."

Cherie all but wrinkled her nose. "People come here to eat?"

"Among Sydney foodies, the inner west has a

reputation for innovative cuisine," Emma pointed out. "Lewisham's still making its mark." That was why she'd chosen to buy in the suburb. With help from the bank, she'd been able to afford the ten-foot-wide single-story cottage that had been squeezed into the garden of the neighboring home several decades ago. The expenses gave her nightmares, but the place itself gave her nothing but satisfaction. And she needed somewhere to live. Besides, this way she only had one mortgage to support.

The previous café had gone broke, but the basic structure had made it easy for Emma to set up her business. After the redecorating she and a group of friends had done, the former café now provided an ideal venue for small dinners, and the sensational food and subdued lighting distracted diners from any flaws in their surroundings. The kitchen was functional enough for these occasions, but wasn't equipped for more ambitious events.

"I don't understand why you're so touchy," Cherie complained. "I'm only trying to help."

"I know, and I appreciate the support."

"Then why react as if I have no right to my opinions?"

*Perhaps because there are so many of them?* "I know you mean well, and I appreciate it. If it wasn't…" *that the client is Nathan Hale?* "…too soon for me to take on big jobs, I'd jump at the chance." Emma crossed her fingers under the desk.

Cherie gestured around them. "You'll never grow by limiting yourself. I was so pleased when you bought this place."

Emma masked her astonishment. "You were?"

"You finally seemed to be getting a sense of direction."

One should always strive for the next goal, Emma had been reminded frequently when she was growing up. And what had been wrong with her sense of direction up to now? Wasn't gaining her diploma in commercial cooking an achievement? Or winning a scholarship to an international food festival in Singapore where she'd worked with world-class chefs? That distinction had earned Emma a job as a junior chef, then she'd skipped a couple of levels to become demi-chef at the Hotel Turista in Sydney's Rocks area. There she'd worked her way up to sous-chef, before deciding to open her own place. "One day I'll get my life on track," she said with an exaggerated sigh.

"Now don't sound so sarcastic. Just because I think your talents could be better utilized doesn't mean I don't appreciate that you have them."

Emma didn't bother trying to unscramble the compliment. Her mother cared about her and her brother, even if she had an annoying way of showing it. "I know, Ma. You and Dad should come to one of my chef's dinners and see how I do things."

Cherie gave her a bright smile. "We'll see."

Code for *a snowball's chance,* Emma knew. What else did she expect? "I'll email you the next few dates."

"Thank you, darling. But we really should discuss Nate's dinner party."

Over her dead body, Emma thought. "Can I get you some coffee and cake? Sophie's baking mini Bakewell tarts with wild huckleberry jam." Distraction didn't only work with customers. She could smell the delicious aroma from here.

Evidently so could her mother. "I'll have a tiny taste," she conceded. "I can work it off at the gym later. Then I want to talk about Nate."

That made one of them.

When Emma went into the kitchen, Sophie shot her a concerned look. "Everything okay?"

"Tell you later," Emma mouthed as she arranged some of the medallion-size tarts on a white plate. She walked over to the commercial coffee machine which came with the building and made two macchiatos, then carried the lot to her office.

Cherie was on the phone and looked up as Emma placed the tray on her desk. "Ah, here she is now. You can talk to her yourself, Nate."

Before Emma could shake her head in protest, the BlackBerry was thrust into her hand. She pulled professionalism around her like a cloak. "Hello, Dr. Hale."

"It was Nate last time, Emma."

No man should have a voice as rich as triple-chocolate fudge brownies, she thought as a shiver of response slid down her spine. And there was a last time? Who knew? "Ah, yes, Nate, we have met."

"And how."

The insinuation sent heat arrowing from her head to her stomach. No, no, this had to stop. Head agreed, body didn't get the memo. "I'm afraid my business isn't fully operational yet," she said. "My mother tells me your birthday is in three weeks, but catering large-scale events isn't an option for at least another three months."

"Saying no isn't an option."

What Dr. Hale wants, Dr. Hale gets. Emma felt a jolt of frustration. No wonder Cherie was so keen on having Emma work for him. Nate and her mother were cut from the same cloth. "Acknowledging limitations isn't failure," she said. "It's a good business practice."

"True, but overcoming those limitations is preferable."

A vision flashed through her mind of Nate facing some huge challenge in the operating room, finding a way around it and saving the patient at the last minute. Wasn't that what always happened with his type? Her father's stories of his heroic interventions had been regular dinner table fare when she was growing up.

"I'll keep your advice in mind," she agreed crisply. "How many guests are you expecting?"

"Fifty at a minimum. I'm thinking of having the party on the terrace—sit-down, of course."

He must have some terrace. A sit-down dinner for fifty would be way off her radar. "Look, Nate, I'll gladly put together some options and email them to you to see if anything I can do meets your requirements." Her tone told him she doubted it would.

"No."

"Just—no?"

"I'd rather discuss this with you face-to-face." She heard the tap of keys as he consulted his schedule. "How does Friday sound?"

"I'm committed on Friday." She had a breakfast meeting with Carla Geering, a talented chef Emma had known since catering college, and Margaret Jennings, a self-taught cook who helped with the chef's dinners once a month. Both were prepared to leave good jobs to join Emma as soon as she was ready. She looked forward to their meetings. All three of them came away inspired and excited about what lay ahead.

But Emma's answer would have been the same whatever day he'd suggested, and she had a feeling he suspected as much.

"I'm sure you can uncommit yourself. I'll see you at my place at eleven."

Just time for her to keep her breakfast date be-

fore seeing him. He reeled off the address, which
she scribbled down, aware of Cherie watching her
keenly.

"Unless you'd like me to pick you up," he added.
"I remember the address."

His tone suggested he remembered far more than
she wanted him to. Was one impulsive action going
to haunt her forever? "I'll find my own way," she said
quickly. Meeting the lion in his den didn't appeal,
either, but it was better than a live-action replay of
a night she would rather not think about. Maybe by
Friday she'd have swine flu and be in quarantine, she
thought. Or maybe she'd be at Nathan Hale's house.
Either way, his catering options wouldn't change, so
he'd have to accept what her business could provide or
find someone else. She knew which she preferred.

Or did she? Wasn't she the slightest bit intrigued
at the prospect of seeing him again? Another thought
struck her. "Will your partner want to participate in
the discussion?" The idea of him living with someone
was surprisingly unsettling.

"No partner, female or male," he informed her,
sounding amused. "Not that the question worried
you last time."

Last time was an aberration, she wanted to say,
but was restrained by her mother listening across the
desk. "We can discuss everything when I see you,"
she said, hoping Nate would get the message.

In the background she heard him being paged. "I

have to go." He sounded reluctant. Imagination, she decided. "I'll look forward to discussing—every-thing—on Friday."

She handed the phone back to her mother. "Happy now?"

Cherie stood up. "Why shouldn't I be? I'm trying to help your business. What made you ask Nate if he has a partner?"

Her mother was like a bloodhound when it came to her daughter and men. "If he'd had one, I'd rather meet with them together. Saves a lot of time and disagreements."

"Not to mention ensuring you're aware of any potential…um…obstacles."

"Nate can have a harem for all I care. This is purely professional."

"Pity." Cherie sounded genuinely disappointed.

"Honestly, Ma, haven't you given up matchmaking by now?"

Her mother's shoulders lifted. "I didn't make you go home with him."

"I didn't go home with him. He gave me a ride, that's all."

"In that case, why so defensive?"

Emma shot her mother a chilly glare. "Telling Dad that if I can't be a doctor I can at least marry one might have something to do with it."

Her brother had shared the information with

Emma, saying he wanted her to be forewarned. Not that the news came as a surprise.

Her mother colored slightly, although media experience kept her body language in check. "Where on earth did you get that idea?"

"Then you don't deny saying it?"

"I can't deny that I'd be pleased to have you carry on the family tradition in some way."

Emma splayed her hands. "Can't you stop being media medico for ten seconds and give me a straight answer? If you're planning on fixing me up with Nate Hale, I'm entitled to know."

"Emma, what's gotten into you? He's having a party. You're a caterer. Why should you suspect me of a hidden agenda?"

"Because I know you. And obviously my choice of career bothers you as much as it ever did."

"Nonsense. I'm proud of both my children."

The same nonanswer Emma had been given when she'd told her parents she'd decided to go to culinary school rather than pursue a career in medicine. A few stints helping out in their practice and at a local nursing home had convinced her she'd rather feed people than minister to their ailments. Cherie had arranged the internship at the nursing home, never suspecting Emma would find her vocation in the facility's kitchen rather than with the residents.

"Didn't you ever want to do anything other than become a doctor?" Emma asked now.

Tucking her phone into her bag, Cherie paused. "How is this relevant?"

Emma already knew the answer. Cherie's father, Emma's grandfather, had helped pioneer bone marrow transplantation. Cherie had grown up hero-worshipping him and took it for granted that she'd follow him into medicine. Not for the first time Emma wondered if her mother had ever questioned her choice. Many years ago, Cherie had painted exquisite miniature landscapes. Perhaps…

Emma killed the thought. No point going there. If life was this hard for her as the family misfit, how much tougher would it have been for her mother, hardwired for conformity since birth? Cherie never stepped on the grass if a sign warned against it, whereas Emma was likely to take off her shoes and run barefoot across it out of sheer devilment. Those genes had to come from Emma's paternal grandmother Jessie Jarrett, a wonderful cook who'd made her mark independently of her oncologist husband. Gramma Jessie was still one of Emma's favorite people.

"Don't worry, Ma. I'll talk to Nate and we'll work something out."

Her mother looked relieved as she came around the desk and dropped a light kiss on Emma's forehead. "You won't regret your decision."

She already regretted it, Emma thought as she saw her mother out. Although she hadn't actually agreed to cater the party, only discuss it. Would she have been so uptight about the meeting if the client wasn't Nate? Probably not. And for that, she had no one to blame but herself.

In the kitchen, her assistant Sophie had finished packing the cold canapés and desserts into insulated containers for their client's cocktail party that evening. Emma double-checked the list, more from habit than because she doubted Sophie, who was always meticulous. "I'm glad they didn't book us to staff tonight's affair. I'll take these around in my car, you lock up and have an early night for once," she said.

Sophie shook her head. "And miss hearing what happened with your mother? No way. I'll make the coffee while you're gone."

Arms laden, Emma turned at the door. "You didn't pack all the Bakewell tarts, did you?"

Sophie gave her a smug smile. "I might have taken out three or four less than perfect ones. Can't send out anything but our best work, can we?"

BY THE TIME EMMA RETURNED fifteen minutes later, Sophie had the coffee made and the tarts plated up. Emma snapped a piece of paper in front of her friend. "The client paid in full on the spot. That should make the bank happy."

Sophie hitched a slender hip onto a stool at the counter. "Good for the bank. Now tell me about your mother's visit. Who's she trying to fix you up with this time?"

Emma affected an air of nonchalance. "What makes you think she's trying to fix me up?"

"Since the day we met in high school, that's all she's been doing. Who is it this time? A psychiatrist who can get to the bottom of your doctor phobia?"

"I don't have a doctor phobia."

"Oh, no?" Sophie pushed her glasses to the end of her nose and mimed holding a pad and pen. "Tell me, Ms. Jarrett, how long have you hated your horse?"

Emma snorted a mouthful of coffee. "I don't have a horse, either."

"You only think you don't have a horse. Come lie on my couch and tell me all about zis problem. I'll lie here beside you. Closeness helps break down zee inhibitions."

Laughing, Emma blotted her shirt front. "My mother doesn't have a psychiatrist lined up for me, thank goodness. She wants us to cater a birthday bash for Nathan Hale."

Sophie pressed a fist against her chest. "The heart surgeon? According to *She Magazine,* he's the sexiest man in medicine. Tell me you said yes."

Emma gestured around the congested kitchen. "Look at this place. How can we take on a sit-down dinner for fifty or more?"

"Charge like a wounded bull, then hire waiters. Some of my study group might help out. They always need cash. Even if his party is on a class night, I can do some of the prep work with you and put in a couple of hours at the venue before going to school."

Sophie was studying for a postgraduate diploma in nutrition and Emma had agreed to work around her commitments, knowing Sophie would be free of them in another few months. Her diploma, which was focused on food services management, would widen the range of services they could offer. Emma bit into a tart. "The upfront expenses will be a stretch. I know they'll be billed back to him, but we'll have to carry the costs till then. The sexiest man in medicine won't settle for anything but the best."

"Ancient Chinese wisdom says Where there's a will, there's a way."

Sophie liked to spout Confucian wisdom whenever possible. Her grandparents had emigrated from Hong Kong to Australia, where their baby girl had grown up and married an Australian sailor, Sophie's dad. "According to you, the only wisdom is ancient Chinese," Emma teased.

"Not at all. There are wise Australian sayings like 'she'll be right' and 'no worries.'"

"True."

"Translated from the original Chinese," Sophie added with a wicked grin.

"No doubt. Was there anything you guys didn't invent?"

"You're just jealous." Sophie leaned forward on

her stool. "Confucius would say It's better to try and fail than not to try at all."

Emma laughed. "Confucius obviously didn't have a kitchen the size of a bathroom."

## CHAPTER TWO

NATE WAS ONLY A CLIENT. She hadn't been herself when they met at her parents' party. Emma repeated the phrases like a mantra as she drove to his place on Friday morning. She was a professional, she could do this. All he had to do was cooperate. Amnesia would also help, she thought.

Nevertheless her fingers twitched at the memory of a dark crew cut crowning a classically shaped head. She'd spent half the party resisting the urge to run her palm over it, until finally she gave in to temptation after finding him tucked in a shadowy corner near the conference room. He'd looked as surprised as she felt, but didn't resist, pressing a kiss to her fingers. When he hadn't shown any inclination to move on to her mouth, she'd taken the initiative, kissing him with increasing enthusiasm as she felt him respond.

"You taste of truffles," he'd murmured when he ended the kiss with what she'd swear had been reluctance.

"Not bad," she'd said, her mind spinning. She'd handled truffle oil hours before, yet he'd still detected the traces on her skin. Had he also noticed the throbbing of her pulse or the racing of her heart in response to his closeness? "What else do you sense?"

He'd looked serious, considering the question before nuzzling her ear with his mouth. "The faintest aura of Paloma perfume. You could drive a man wild with those two scents."

Tingles like faint electrical impulses had swept through her and she'd pressed closer to him. She found his long, lean body attractive. He had wide shoulders, narrow hips, a long neck and strong jawline faintly shaded by stubble. Urbane and sexily volatile.

"Am I driving you wild?" she asked. He was definitely having an impact on her.

"Mmm-hmm. Imagine what you could do if you were sober."

She'd recoiled as if stung. "I'm not drunk. All I've had to drink is one glass of wine and one orange juice."

"With a generous slug of vodka added by your brother."

"Oh, no, he wouldn't." The muzziness in her brain started to make sense. "I'll kill him."

"You didn't ask him to make you a mixer?"

She shook her head. After starting work at 4:00 a.m. and not stopping to eat lunch, she'd been too tired to have more than one alcoholic drink, knowing the effect it was likely to have on her. "Must be his idea of a joke. You'd think with all his degrees and experience, he'd know better."

"They don't give degrees in common sense."

Using Nate for leverage she'd straightened, aware of her head spinning. She was clinging to him like a demented sex kitten. What must he think of her?

But all he'd said was, "I'm on call so often that I don't drink a lot. I'll take a rain check on driving you wild and drive you home instead."

She still wasn't sure why she let him, because she'd had to listen to a lecture about keeping an eye on drinks even at a private party. In a low-slung Branxton sports car that she'd struggled to get into with some degree of grace, he drove fast but in control.

Her head pounded. "I'm sorry for trying to jump your bones. This is the first time I've had a spiked drink."

"Hopefully also the last. Another man could easily have taken advantage of your…enthusiasm."

"But saintly medicos like you wouldn't dream of doing such a thing."

He'd looked at her curiously. "What does my work have to do with this?"

"According to my parents, doctors have to set a good example for the rest of us."

He made a point of slowing down, even though he was well within the limit, and smiled over at her. "Better not be stopped for speeding."

"Don't worry. As soon as the officer sees the title

on your license, he'll assume you're rushing to some medical emergency."

"Is that why you threw yourself at me?" He sounded amused by the turn the conversation was taking. "You fancy a man with a title?"

"I've been surrounded by men and women with medical titles all my life. It's not a novelty." She didn't like being reduced to the status of doctor groupie. "In my experience, more than a few doctors are walking, talking egos with delusions of godhood."

"That's a sweeping judgment, isn't it? You were the one who came on to me, remember?"

Remember? Her skin still felt hot and tight. She knew she'd never forget this night as long as she lived. "I'm well aware of the fact," she said, enunciating carefully. She really did feel horribly unwell. Throwing up on his immaculate leather upholstery would be the last straw, but she would not ask him to pull over so she could humiliate herself even more by the side of the road. "We've agreed the vodka didn't help. At least that's my excuse. What's yours?"

"Do I need one?"

"You didn't resist when I touched you."

"Pushing you away would have attracted more attention than I thought you'd want."

"You don't have a clue what I want." Liar, she told herself. She'd been attracted to him from the moment she saw him walk into the party as if he owned it.

"I can guess what you want. But one, you're too

young. Two, you've had more to drink than is good
for you. And three, your parents are my colleagues.
I wouldn't hurt them by taking advantage of their
daughter."

But it was okay to hurt her, she thought bitterly.
She chose the only thing on his list she could legiti-
mately challenge. "For your information, I'm twenty-
eight."

He shot her a sideways glance. "My mistake. I
took you for a decade younger."

"I've always looked younger than I am. Ma says
I'll be glad one day, but it's a pain having to show ID
whenever I go out at night."

"Your mother's right."

"At least I sound like my generation," she said,
tiring of him siding with her parents. "You can't be
that many years older than me."

"Wiser, maybe."

"Yes, the doctor ego thing."

"Don't forget the delusions of godhood," he said.
"You have me typecast, but you haven't told me what
you do for a living."

"I'm a qualified chef."

"You're not in medicine?"

She'd slid down a little in the leather seat of his
beautiful car. "Nope. Sad, isn't it?"

"Only sad if you wanted to and couldn't."

"I didn't want to. I'm creating a new branch of the
Jarrett family."

"Good for you. Is this your place?"

His voice gave no clue what he thought of the run-down house that was both home and business. "Mine and the bank's."

"I'll walk you in."

"No need." Her keys were already in her hand. She was embarrassed enough for one night without him seeing the dilapidated former café she was slowly turning into a boutique eatery. She couldn't do the renovations she wanted until the business brought in more money, and the small apartment she lived in at the rear wasn't a priority.

He came around to her side of the car and opened the door. "I'll wait until you're safely inside."

He sounded as if he doubted she could make it under her own steam. With good reason, she found as soon as the night air hit her. She concentrated on getting the front door open and herself inside without stumbling, sighing with relief when she closed the door behind her and leaned against it. After a few minutes, she heard him start his car and drive away.

Had she really said doctors were walking egos with delusions of godhood? Thinking it was one thing, but saying it... She'd kill Todd for spiking that drink. But was it all his fault? Hadn't the vodka provided the excuse to do exactly what she'd wanted to do from her first sight of Nate? That didn't let her brother off the hook, but she knew she had to take some responsibility. She should have kept a better eye on her drink. But like hypnotism, alcohol couldn't make her behave totally out of character. So what did tonight say about her?

Despite Nate's lecture and his patronizing manner, the memory of his bristly hair under her hand elicited a shiver of desire she couldn't blame on anything but sexual attraction. And his designer stubble had felt so enticing when she kissed him. He'd turned her on, even as she'd turned him off. She'd resolved never to willingly cross his path again.

And now she was walking up to his front door.

SHE SHOULD HAVE EXPECTED a man like Nate to do things his own way. Instead of meeting her in an office or at least a living room, he was waiting for her in a garden arbor overgrown with old-fashioned white roses. When his housekeeper led her to him, the scent of the flowers made her feel light-headed. She refused to believe Nate himself could have such an effect on her. "Thanks, Joanna," she said, but the woman had already turned back toward the house.

Emma hadn't seen Nate since the ill-fated Christmas party but his height and athletic build were fixed in her memory. If anything, he looked even more attractive in daylight. He stood up as she climbed the steps into the arbor. His eyes, which had shone amber under artificial light, now glinted with gold flecks around the iris. In narrow-cut jeans, a pale blue

T-shirt with random French phrases scribbled across the front and bare feet thrust into leather sandals, he looked more like a university student than a successful surgeon. She immediately felt overdressed in her businesslike taupe pants and short black cardigan with a lacy white camisole.

He stuck out his hand. "Good to see you again, Emma."

With an assurance she was far from feeling, she touched her palm to his, but before she could step away and sit down at the wooden table strewn with papers, his grip tightened and he pulled her closer.

"Nate, what are you doing? This isn't a good idea." She was aware of how unconvincing the words sounded.

He gestured with his free hand. "You can't tell me you felt more romantic in a boardroom setting than in a rose garden?"

"I didn't feel romantic at all. That was the vodka talking."

His warm gaze met hers. "*Only* the vodka?"

Alarmed at how tempting his mouth looked, she held still with an effort. "You know it was."

And she should have known enough to stay away from him. She felt her resistance slipping even now as he slid his hand down to the small of her back. His touch was light. She could have broken the contact with the slightest move. So why didn't she? "I came here to discuss catering arrangements for your party, not for…this."

"You're right," he said, moving away with every sign of reluctance. "I've been thinking about that night. Seeing you here now made me want to find out if what I remembered about our encounter was real."

"The encounter wasn't real, at least not in the way you mean," she assured him, sitting down at the table. "And it won't happen again."

His expression was devilish as he sat opposite her. "Are you sure it won't? I'm not."

The thought that she disturbed his equilibrium gave her a moment of satisfaction before she squelched it. "We should get down to business?"

"Coward," he murmured so softly she couldn't be sure she'd heard him. The ring tone of a cell phone cut off any retort she might have made. The Chipmunks' "Witch Doctor," she noticed. So the man had a sense of humor.

He shot her an apologetic look as he flipped the phone open and glanced at the number. "The hospital," he said to her. "Hale speaking."

An all too familiar sensation crept over her. *The hospital.* How many of her family's activities had been interrupted by those same words? When she was a child, the reasons her parents had to take the calls had been explained to her over and over again.

The clear message she'd received was that patients were more important than she was.

Whether it was a school play, a sporting event, a graduation, or simply a time when she needed their support, her parents would promise to get there as soon as they could. Medical duties came first. Often they wouldn't get to her event at all, or she'd solve the problem by herself. The upside was she'd developed a healthy self-reliance. The downside was a reluctance to depend on other people, or expect them to be there for her.

But all this was in the past. Replaying her grievances because Nate had answered a call from the hospital didn't change anything. She heard him give a string of instructions concerning a patient's treatment, sounding so self-assured that she imagined the person at the other end standing at attention. Her father and mother sounded exactly the same.

He ended the call and placed the phone on the table. "I hope you gave your brother hell for spiking your drink."

"You bet I did." Todd had admitted he'd drunk too much himself, falling over himself to apologize. She'd never seen her brother so upset. "I don't think he'll do anything that idiotic again." Emma hoped she could say the same for herself.

Nate nodded. "Would you like some iced tea?"

A carafe and glasses sat on a tray on a little table and he poured a glass for her. Ice tinkled in a tube in the center of the carafe, chilling the drink without diluting it. "Unusual flavor," she said after taking a sip.

"Pomegranate, from a tree growing in the garden."

Pleasure rippled through her. Her grandmother also grew the fruit, and had included some recipes in one of her cookbooks. Emma would have to look them up.

She opened her net book and swiveled the screen toward him. "As I told you on the phone, my business isn't fully up to speed yet, but I've put together a selection of menus that might—"

His phone rang again and he held up a hand to silence her as he took the call. This time he didn't need to say it was the hospital. He listened intently then unleashed a string of commands. "Do you need me there?" he asked.

If anything was guaranteed to kill her interest in him, leaving her sitting while he took off would do the trick. Once upon a time she'd let herself be guilt-tripped into feeling selfish for putting her needs ahead of someone in crisis, until she realized that there would always be another crisis, and not even the most highly qualified doctor was indispensable. There was always someone to help, whereas she had only one family. The problem was convincing her parents that she had as much right to their time as their patients did.

He put the phone down again. "Coming from a medical family, you'd be used to interruptions," he said.

"Yes, I am."

The coldness she couldn't keep out of her voice made him raise an eyebrow, but he didn't respond. Instead he scrolled through the document she'd sat up late last night preparing for him. "Impressive," he said. "The combinations are nicely balanced. Tarte Tatin is one of my favorites. Making it with figs and leeks is an interesting variation."

She heard what he didn't say. "But?"

"These options are a bit ordinary."

Pride made her bristle but she kept herself in check. "Not everyone appreciates the unusual when it comes to food."

"My guests will. A group of us belong to a private gourmet club that travels the country for new and interesting eating experiences."

"What kind of experiences?" she asked. Her mother might have mentioned he and his friends were gourmands.

His eyes brightened. "There's a tiny place in Rosebud on the Mornington Peninsula in Victoria. Only holds twenty people, and everything they serve comes from their own produce or is sourced locally. We flew down there one Sunday, spent a day with the owners, picking ingredients from their kitchen garden, helping with preparation and eating one of the best meals of my life. Another time, we traveled to the outback to eat crocodile meat beside a river infested with them."

"Hardly a relaxing venue," she said, wondering how often he'd been interrupted by work calls there.

He leaned forward. "That's the point. Knowing we were dining on a man-eater in its territory was a real buzz. The indigenous community hosting the dinner obtain all the ingredients in and around the river. They supplied the crocodile meat and showed us how to hunt goannas, dig for yams and climb trees to harvest wild honey." He brought his fingertips together. "Have you eaten live witchetty grubs?"

She couldn't suppress a shudder. "It's not high on my list of foods to try."

His lopsided grin was oddly appealing. "You should. The texture is soft, and the taste reminiscent of a gamey veal pâté. You hold the grub by the head and kind of suck the meat off." He mimed the action.

"Are you telling me you'd like live grubs on your birthday menu?"

He shook his head. "Only a few of the group volunteered for that experience. But generally we're more adventurous with food than most people, so you can pull out all the stops."

His proposal was a chef's dream, but she was in

no position to take advantage of it while she was still in the throes of establishing her business.

She closed the net book. "I can't tell you how much this tempts me." In more ways than one, she thought, wondering fleetingly if she was turning the job down because of the business or him. "In good conscience, I won't take a job on unless I can do it well. Now I know what you're looking for, I'm positive I'm not the right person for this assignment."

"And I'm positive that you are."

He wasn't insisting because of her talents, but because he was used to getting his own way. She'd been through similar scenes with her family. His attitude on the phone had shown her how accustomed he was to being in charge.

"Why are you so determined to hire Love This Catering?" she asked. "You must have a lot of contacts in the food business through your group."

He took his time answering. "You intrigue me. I know your parents and brother professionally, and you're totally different from them."

"In what way?" she asked warily, so used to being compared with her family and found wanting that she braced herself automatically.

"You're an original," he said, surprising her. "You don't like being reminded of how you came on to me at the party, but no one's done anything like that to me before, at least not so ingenuously. The alcohol may have boosted your nerve, but it didn't put the idea in your head. You saw what you wanted and you went after it. Just as you did when you started your own business."

"I get my passion for cooking from my grandmother, Jessie Jarrett," she explained, reluctantly pleased by his appreciation.

He frowned. "I thought all your family were doctors."

"Dad's father is an oncologist, but Gramma Jessie is better known for writing cookbooks."

"I worked with Greg Jarrett Sr. during my residency," Nate mused. He showed no interest in Jessie's activities, Emma noted without surprise.

"And the Kenners?" he prompted.

She gave a sigh. "Trudy Kenner met my grandfather when they were both in a civilian surgical and medical team during the Vietnam War. You might have heard of him—Howard Kenner."

"I'm familiar with his work in antirejection therapy for transplant patients," Nate said. "Your mother goes by Kenner-Jarrett, but I didn't make the connection."

"She'd probably be glad to introduce you." Emma knew how proud Cherie was of her father. "He travels overseas a lot and we don't see much of him, but he's due back in Australia next month."

"He might be here in time for the party," Nate observed.

"You never know your luck." Emma felt cheated.

For a few brief minutes, he'd seen her as an individual instead of a member of a medical dynasty, and a misfit at that.

She gathered her things together. "Since none of my menus is to your liking, I'd better get back to the drawing board."

His hand closed over hers, and it took an effort not to jerk away. "There's nothing wrong with your menus. I'm sure your clients love them all. And I saw your eyes light up when I asked you to prepare something extraordinary for me, so the problem isn't the challenge. Something else I said got your back up. What is it?"

"Isn't my lack of facilities enough reason to turn you down?"

He shook his head. "You strike me as the type of cook who can perform miracles with a campfire if you have to. Something else is bugging you."

*He* was bugging her, but she didn't say so. "I don't like being railroaded."

He withdrew his hand. "By a walking ego with delusions of godhood," he finished for her.

"You said it this time, not me."

"You were thinking it."

The last thing she wanted him knowing was how conflicted he made her feel. Half of her wanted to walk away to avoid dealing with his world and all the negatives it represented in her life. The other half insisted on remembering how it felt to kiss him. She kept her voice level. "I'm entitled to my thoughts."

"Of course." He nodded tightly. "What do you think Jessie would do?"

Amazed that the name had registered with him when Jessie's cookbooks were so far beneath his notice, she said warily, "Why do you ask?"

"She was the odd one out in her family, yet she's a success in her own right. She didn't let herself be overshadowed by a well-known husband."

"Jessie is one of a kind."

"What about Trudy Kenner? She practiced medicine in a war zone alongside her husband. And not your mother."

"Only me," she said under her breath.

He heard anyway. "There's one way you can trump them if you choose. Make such a success of what you do that they end up living in *your* shadow."

She almost choked with suppressed laughter. The idea of Cherie being described as Emma Jarrett's mother instead of the other way around was as unlikely as it was appealing. She imagined a TV interviewer asking Cherie, "What's it like having a culinary genius in the family?"

Nate's phone rang. He turned slightly away and rattled off instructions, then closed the phone. "This time I have to go. Can I drop you somewhere?"

Reality check, she thought. She'd almost let herself believe he was different, understanding her passion instead of dismissing it. "I drove here, I'm sure I'll remember the way back."

His gaze softened. "Good, I wouldn't want you to forget. Take your time finishing your drink. Then Joanna will show you around the kitchen. I'll drop by your office next Tuesday after work. That should give you time to put together a menu to knock my socks off. We both know you want to."

Without giving her the chance to contradict him, he bounded down the steps and headed toward the house, taking for granted that she'd do exactly what he wanted.

In spite of her annoyance, the challenge primed her senses like an explosive charge. How had he known? she wondered as she finished the pomegranate tea. He'd zeroed in on the one thing that guaranteed her cooperation, the chance to show that she was as first-rate in her world as the rest of her family was in theirs. Her feelings had nothing to do with the way Nate's touch affected her, or how tempted she was to kiss him again. This was purely professional. Or so she tried to assure herself.

As NATE DROVE TO THE HOSPITAL, his mind grappled with the complications his team had reported about one of their patients. Normally, he'd have options mapped out by the time he got there, but his thoughts were distracted by his meeting with the lovely Emma.

She didn't want anything to do with him, so why was he determined to have her mastermind his celebration dinner? Was he so used to his team jumping when he snapped his fingers that he'd forgotten how to handle rejection? He hated to think so, and yet… he felt an attraction for Emma Jarrett that he couldn't pin down, like the first taste of a weird and wonderful food. He craved more of her while suspecting she wouldn't be good for him. She didn't like him. She didn't like doctors, he corrected. Hardly surprising given the way her family regarded her choice of career. When Cherie had heard Nate's assistant joshing him about his upcoming birthday and asking what he was doing about a party, she'd recommended Emma, but had made far more of her daughter's single status than her catering skills.

Cherie was wasting her time matchmaking. Nate hadn't missed the way Emma frowned every time he took a call this morning, or the flicker of frustration when he announced he had to go to the hospital. He'd been through it all before in his own family.

When his mother could no longer stand the round-the-clock demands of his father's country medical practice, she'd carted twelve-year-old Nate back to Sydney, eventually moving them in with her lawyer. She and Josh were still a couple. His father, coming up to retirement age, was the country town's only doctor and worked much longer hours than he preferred. He had never remarried.

Three years ago, Nate had been practically engaged to Pamela Coyne, a stunningly beautiful journalist who'd turned his mates green with envy. Hot in every way a woman could be hot, she'd run cold after finding herself attending too many functions alone because he'd been called away by an emergency. The final showdown had been ugly, but short of abandoning his life's work, Nate couldn't see anything changing. A doctor's life was what it was. Eventually Pam had told him what he could do with his medical degree, and was now living with a stockbroker.

After so many years as an only child, Nate had been surprised when his mother presented him with a half brother, Luke, now fifteen. The gulf between their ages meant Nate felt more like an uncle to Luke, and they didn't have much in common. Luke was into skateboarding, fast cars and music Nate thought barely qualified for the name. The teenager stayed away from school when he felt like it, and hung out with a group that worried his parents. Nate had tried talking to Luke man-to-man, but the gap was too wide. Nate had always envied large families and hoped to have one of his own. But the mother of his kids would have to come from the medical world and understand its pressures. With his thirty-fifth birthday fast approaching, the prospects weren't looking good.

He hadn't exactly been a lone wolf. He'd had his share of romances, parting without too many regrets on either side when the relationship ran its course. Now that he thought about it, he was shocked to realize that there'd been no romance in his life for nearly three months. No wonder he'd reacted so strongly to having Emma come on to him at that Christmas party.

Abstinence was his problem, not Emma, he decided, muttering as a white SUV cut in front of him. Who was he kidding? Only after meeting her had the craving for a lasting relationship really set in. It wasn't only sex he needed. He wanted a sense of home and family, the stuff hardest to come by. Kids might be too busy to meet dad at the door any more, and wives kept equally long hours as their partners did, but they could still be a team. The SUV stopped for a red light. A yellow tag in the rear window read Family on Board. How would it feel to have a sign like that in his car?

He drummed his palms against the steering wheel in frustration. Turning thirty-five was getting to him. He should go out with Emma, take her to bed and enjoy the experience until one of them moved on. The fear that he might not want to stopped him. She was definitely the wrong candidate. He'd seen too many danger signals already. Hands off was the only safe policy, even though the idea clashed with his instincts like a misdiagnosis.

## CHAPTER THREE

SOPHIE STUCK HER HEAD around Emma's office door on Tuesday morning. "Are you in for phone calls yet? I've had six inquiries so far and two new clients wanting to book events. One of them's a wedding a year from now."

"The Nathan Hale effect?"

"Yup. Word's getting around." Sophie carried in Emma's Garfield mug. "Chai latte. I thought you'd appreciate it."

"Thanks." Emma cleared a small space to let Sophie put the cup down among the recipe books, cards and handwritten notes swamping her computer. "You'd think my mother would wait until we've done the job before telling everyone she knows."

Another mug in hand, Sophie sat down. "No pressure."

Emma sipped her tea. "It doesn't help that Nate's closest friends have either cooked or eaten some of the best meals in the world. I looked up his gourmet group online and two Michelin-starred chefs are members. How do you think they'd like white truffle donuts and basil-infused snails?"

"About as much as I would." Sophie linked her hands on the desk. "I prefer the food my Chinese grandmother makes, simple but delicious. A few fresh ingredients, mostly from her garden, although she draws the line at snails. To her the main thing is all of us sharing the meal. Although that's probably nostalgia speaking."

With Garfield halfway to her mouth, Emma froze, staring at Sophie. "Nostalgia—that's the answer! Soph, you're a genius."

Sophie gave her a measured look. "O-kay. I mean, you're right about the genius part, but what did I say this time?"

Ignoring the recipe cards and papers showering the floor as she moved, Emma leaned forward. "Remember I told you about seeing Nate's kitchen after our meeting last Friday?" Not waiting for Sophie's nod, she plunged on. "It's the kind I dream of putting in here—acres of stainless steel work surfaces, the latest Italian appliances, refrigerators big enough to live in. You could run a restaurant from his kitchen. And you know what?"

"No, what?"

"He hardly sets foot in the place."

"Doesn't he employ a cook?"

Emma shook her head. "Joanna, his housekeeper, says cooking isn't in her job description, and he doesn't have any other staff. She told me he eats out almost every night, or has a restaurant deliver.

The most he ever does is put together a snack or a sandwich for himself in the butler's pantry, which is practically another kitchen."

"What a waste. But knowing this solves his catering problem how?"

Emma stood up, her efforts to pace hampered by the papers on the floor, so she sat down again. "I did some research on our Dr. Hale." She didn't add it was as much for her own interest as to get an idea of his lifestyle. "His parents split up when he was twelve. His dad is a country doctor living alone, and his mother lives in Sydney with her partner and their fifteen-year-old son."

"Sounds fairly typical," Sophie observed. "You and I are the minority these days with two parents still married and living in the same house."

"Exactly my point," Emma went on. "We all want what we don't have."

"Including Dr. Hale." Sophie sounded as if she was starting to understand.

"You got it. By chasing exotic foods and recipes, I'd be giving Nate what he already has, when I should be giving him what he *doesn't* have."

"Meals like Mama used to make."

"Except his mama never made them. If his life was like the family of most country doctors—or city ones for that matter—his father missed more meals than he showed up for. Or they'd sit down to eat when his father was home, then be interrupted by calls. Being dragged out at all hours would be normal." Emma knew she was talking about her own family as much as Nate's.

Sophie got her drift. "And when they moved to Sydney, his mother was working, providing for them both. I'm thinking pizzas and fast food."

Emma dragged her fingers through her hair, spiking it. "No wonder he likes exotic foods now. And going out to eat must feel more normal than family dinners around a big table."

Sophie grinned. "Is that what you're thinking of giving him for his birthday?"

"You betcha. I'm picturing wonderful homemade dishes, big bowls of fluffy mashed potatoes, fruit and ice cream and rum babas with cream. How long is it since you had rum baba?"

"A long time. I used to think they were so sophisticated because of the alcohol oozing out of them." Sophie tilted her head to one side. "At least we'll have heart specialists on hand. This plan sounds decadent enough to send you straight to the cardiac ward."

Emma shook her head. "Food can taste decadent without the artery damage. We could create the family dining experience by making grown-up versions of all that comfort food."

"Aren't you forgetting something?"

Emma couldn't see what. "It's perfect, I know it is."

"The idea is brilliant, but who's going to produce

this bounty? I can help you with the prep work ahead of time, and I'll be on the spot for the first hour, but I have an important oral exam I can't skip. Carla's working that night, and Margaret will be in Bali, so they can't help. You'll be doing the lion's share of the work on your own."

Emma spread her hands. "I can't *not* do it, Soph. You said yourself we're getting inquiries purely because word of mouth has us working with Nathan Hale. Can you imagine what will happen once we actually deliver the goods?"

"The business will go from struggling to booming," Sophie said. "Why couldn't this chance have come up *after* I finished my course?"

"Murphy's Law. We'll manage somehow." Emma spoke with a confidence she was far from feeling. "If you don't need me in the kitchen, I'll turn this harebrained scheme into a workable proposal to show Nate when he comes here later today."

Sophie stood up. "I can manage, thanks. I've finished prepping lunch for the lady bowlers. Plenty of time before I have to deliver everything to their club room. What can I do to help?"

"You can contact some furniture rental places and find out what it would cost to rent a stack of big, old-fashioned dining tables and chairs." Emma's mind was racing. "The chairs wouldn't have to match. In fact it's better if they don't. They should look like they came straight out of Grandma's dining room. I'll include the costs in the budget for Nate's approval."

"On it, boss." Sophie sounded excited. "Where are you going to get the nostalgic recipes?"

"I don't have to look far for inspiration." Emma rummaged among the pile of books on her desk and came up with the one she wanted. "*Jessie's Kitchen*, by Jessica Jarrett."

Handling the well-thumbed book bathed Emma in happy memories. As a little girl visiting her grandmother, she had enjoyed many of the foods described in the book. As well as her own recipes, Jessie had included some her mother and grandmother had handed down to her, creating a fifty-year history of family food, studded with anecdotes of her life as a young mother on the outskirts of Sydney. Early in their marriage, Jessie and her husband had lived not far from East Hills, then the last stop on the suburban railway line. Their house was set in the middle of acres of rugged bush between East Hills and Heathcote.

The book fell open at Jessie's never-fail sponge cake recipe and Emma's mouth watered, recalling the feathery lightness of the cake filled with cream and Jessie's home-made strawberry jam, the top cloudy with icing sugar. Gramma had given her a big wedge of the cake as consolation for getting lost in the bush. Emma had been picking flowers when a bee flew at her. She'd screamed and run, not stopping until she stumbled into a shallow creek, splashing water around to scare the bee away. Only then did she realize she didn't know the way back.

Remembering how the branches of the eucalyptus trees had reached for her like ghostly arms could still make her shudder. She'd tried walking back to the house, but went round in circles, always returning to the creek.

She'd never felt more relieved to hear her father calling her name. He'd been so angry, she was almost sorry she'd answered, but the sun was setting and she was afraid to spend the night alone by the creek. Without a word, he'd carried her back to Gramma's house and sat her down on a stool in the kitchen. Gramma and Cherie had fussed, but Emma's father had silenced them with his gruff doctor's voice as he tended to her scratches and bruises.

"She's fine, aren't you, girlie?" he'd asked when he finished.

There was only one answer he wanted to hear. "Yes, Daddy."

He'd patted her shoulder. "Good. You won't go running off and getting lost in the bush again, will you?"

Not if it meant getting such a cold reception. When she was found, her fantasy of cuddles and warmth in tatters, she'd promised herself to be more careful next time. She'd rather have a bee sting her nearly to death than make her father that angry with her.

Gramma Jessie's compassion had eased some of

Emma's wretchedness. "Give the child a break, Greg, she's only four." She'd lifted Emma off the stool. "You sit at the table and I'll get you some sponge cake. And you," she said, glaring at Emma's parents, "might like to help yourself to something from the cocktail cabinet."

Emma ate her cake and the homemade lemon drink her gramma served her in the brightly lit kitchen, surrounded by delicious cooking smells and an atmosphere of warmth, while Jessie had sat across the table from her and listened to her adventure.

Realizing she was stroking the book's cover, Emma let her hand fall to her lap. Was it any wonder she'd rejected her parents' world in favor of her grandmother's? As she grew older, she'd come to understand that being in medicine meant walling off many of your own feelings in order to do your job. She admired her parents and brother for their lifesaving skills, but surely life wasn't only about clinical survival? What about emotional well-being? Maybe it was up to people like Jessie and Emma to balance out the medical side with their own form of caring. "There's room in Heaven for all kinds of angels," Emma remembered Jessie telling her one day when she asked why she was the only one in her family who had a problem with the sight of blood. The answer had puzzled her for a long time, but now she knew exactly what Jessie had meant.

Nate was a doctor, she reminded herself. Would

he appreciate what she wanted to do for his birthday dinner? There was one way to find out. She pulled her keyboard toward her and went to work.

FEELING HER BACK MUSCLES complaining, Emma stretched and glanced at her watch, startled to see how much time had passed. There was no sound from the kitchen. Sophie had a lecture this afternoon, and had probably gone straight there after delivering the food to the bowling club. Emma realized she was hungry and headed for the kitchen, where she made herself a chicken wrap, eating it standing at a bench, imagining the room with the new fixtures and fittings in place. Why couldn't Nate's birthday be a few months later? Then she could have really shown him what she could do.

It wasn't as if Emma cared about impressing Nate. He'd been quick enough to leave her with his housekeeper after their meeting. She was lucky he was making time to see her today.

At least she thought he'd suggested today. Emma checked her diary. The date was right. So where was Dr. Hale? She hesitated a moment then called his cell phone.

After several rings, she began mentally composing a message for his voice mail when a masculine voice snapped, "Hale speaking."

"Nate, it's Emma Jarrett."

"Emma?" He sounded a million miles away. "Did

we have a date tonight?" Before she could reply, he
said, "Oh, hell, you're not that Emma, are you?"

Tension gripped Emma. Who was *that* Emma?
Someone he'd dated, or possibly still did? Not that
*this* Emma cared. She said coolly, "You requested a
meeting at my office today to review ideas for your
party."

This wasn't about him as a man, she reminded
herself tautly. This was business.

"I did?" he asked vaguely. "Look, something came
up. I'm going to be another hour or so."

In the medical world, something always came up.
"I can email you my notes and prices if you prefer,"
she said, trying not to let him hear her disappointment. She'd looked forward to sharing his enthusiasm
for her plans. And seeing him again. She swiftly suppressed the thought.

She heard his muffled voice as he spoke to someone else, then he came back on the line. "No need.
How about I pick you up at your place as soon as I
can get away?"

The increased beating of her heart irritated her,
sharpening her tone. "And go where?" If he thought
she was having dinner with him, only to be interrupted constantly by his relentless cell phone, he was
out of luck.

"I'll let you know when I get there," he said.

Before she could demand more details, he'd
hung up.

Her knuckles whitened around the phone as an all too familiar feeling washed over her. How many times had she been left dangling by her family when something had come up? She resisted the urge to slam the phone down. If Nate thought she'd wait for him to spare her a few crumbs of his attention, she had news for him.

She printed out her proposal, copied the pages to disk and slid the lot into one of the monogrammed folders she'd had made up when she started the business. Placing the folder into a large envelope, she scrawled his name on the outside. Then she called a cab and gave Nate's address and the envelope to the driver. As soon as they were gone, she sat down, feeling drained. But there was one more step to take.

She texted Nate to say she was unable to move their appointment, but the information he needed was on its way. He could get back to her when he was ready. Then she surveyed her chaotic office. She should tidy up before retreating to her flat at the back of the building, but couldn't muster the enthusiasm and closed the door on the mess. It would still be there tomorrow.

An hour later, wearing her favorite sleeveless top and track pants and a well-worn pair of running shoes, she'd barely sat down to work on the velvet evening bag she was making for Sophie's birthday when the doorbell rang. The business facade of the building deterred most door-to-door salespeople. Had

Sophie forgotten something? If so, why didn't she come around the back?

But when Emma checked the peephole, instead of her friend waiting in the street, she found Nate Hale leaning against the door frame, his hand raised to press the bell again. As she opened the door, she felt her heart kick against her ribs. "You're lucky to catch me still here."

He looked skeptical. "Going out?"

She knew her workout clothes argued against a hot date. "I sent you a text saying I couldn't reschedule our meeting."

"Yet you're still here."

He was reading her like a book and she didn't enjoy it. "I had some things to do first." Her tone said it was none of his business.

He refused to get the message. "I came to apologize in person."

Heat spun through her. "That's not necessary."

He shifted his stance so one arm reached over her head to grip the door frame, locking her in place. "Don't you mean not expected from a walking ego?"

This close, he was affecting her more than she liked. It wasn't only the sculpted chest outlined by a bad-boy muscle shirt and the snugly fitting jeans that were sending her imagination soaring. He had come to apologize, something so rare in her experience that she hardly knew how to respond. She hid behind a cliché. "The customer is always right."

Wrong approach, she thought when his mouth curved into a smile. "Finally we agree on something."

Her suspicion flared. "Why do I feel as if I'm being set up?"

His look was all innocence, difficult to carry off given his rebel looks, but somehow he managed it. "You want to discuss your proposal, I'm all ears. But not here. I need some air, and you look like you do, too."

Her hand went to her hair before she stopped the movement. "Careful, you might give me a swollen head."

"It's not a criticism, merely an observation. I'll bet this is the first time you've stepped outside all day."

"Wrong." She didn't add that the only other time had been to give his package to the cab driver. "So you can drop the doorstep diagnostics."

"Believe me, I'm too beat to diagnose anything right now except my need to move and stretch."

Curiosity won. "You want me to come for a walk with you?"

"We can settle our business while we're out. Why not kill two birds with one stone?"

Disappointed to find his invitation was aimed at saving time rather than a wish to be with her, she hid her reaction. She knew how his world worked. Or she should by now. She turned, trying not to collide with his hard body. "I'll get my purse."

"You don't need it. Is everything locked up inside?"

She nodded and showed him the keys clipped to her belt. "I only have to set the alarm and I'm ready."

Not true, she knew, as she tapped the security code into the panel inside the front door. She'd have preferred talking business with her desk between them. Several rooms would have been even better, she thought. Sending her proposal by cab had been an act of cowardice to avoid the attraction she felt whenever he came near her. Nothing could come of it. Nothing good, anyway.

*Best laid plans,* she told herself as she pulled the front door shut.

He was holding his car door open. "I thought you wanted to walk," she said. What was he up to?

He slid into the driver's seat. "We're only driving as far as Canada Bay. Have you done the bay walk?"

Sophie had been nagging her to try it. "Not so far."

"You're in for a treat."

The sun was low and the temperature pleasantly mild by the time he parked the car on Henley Marine Drive near the Iron Cove Bridge. Emma sniffed the salty air. He was right. She was glad to be out of the office, but sorry the walk was a means to an end for him. Reminding herself that her business was already gaining clients on the strength of her connection with him, she set herself to match his long strides along a wide footpath around the mangrove-lined foreshores of the cove.

She would have liked to stop and read the signs about the flora and fauna in the surrounding bay, but Nate set a demanding pace that left little time to admire the scenery as it shifted between city skyline and thick greenery. Most of Emma's workouts were in a gym, accompanied by music with a throbbing beat. She wasn't out of shape, but neither was she in his league, although she was damned if she'd let him outclass her.

When had this walk become a competition? she wondered. But then her whole life had been one long competition with the medical fraternity on one side and herself on the other. This was only the latest installment.

"Ready for a break? We're about halfway," he said, steering her to a park marked by a large sandstone cross at the top. From here she could see the city of Sydney and waterways all the way to Rodd Island. He dropped to the grass and wrapped his arms around his bent knees, taking in the view.

She sat down beside him, careful to keep a safe distance. He unclipped a water bottle from his belt and handed it to her. She drank, aware that his lips would soon touch the same spot as hers. Almost like a kiss.

And she knew exactly how that felt, an inner voice whispered. The hard contours of his mouth, the rasp of stubble against her cheek, the wine-rich taste of his breath were all burned into her memory.

The thought made her frown. She'd known spending too much time with him was a risk. Their worlds were too different. Getting involved with a high-flying surgeon like Nate was playing with fire, and she had no intention of getting burned.

Jumping to her feet, she handed him back the water bottle. "I should get moving."

"What's your hurry?"

"It will be dark soon" was her lame excuse.

"Don't you feel safe with me?"

Physically perhaps, but not where her peace of mind was concerned. "You might be missed," she said. "I'm surprised your cell phone hasn't rung by now."

He rose in one lithe movement. "My phone's set to vibrate. My assistant knows how to get hold of me, and then only if there's a crisis she can't handle."

Emma couldn't hide her disbelief. To her parents and brother, every call was a crisis only they could handle. Confusion coiled through her, followed by annoyance. He'd seen how irritated she'd been over the constant interruptions to their meeting at his house. Was this a new strategy to get his own way, or was something else going on here?

She planted her hands on her hips. "This won't work."

"What won't?"

"Provided we can agree on the details, I'll cater your party because it's in both our interests, but that's all."

He frowned. "What else do you think I want?"

She dragged in a deep breath. "Isn't it obvious? Me."

## CHAPTER FOUR

WHAT THE HELL? STANDING IN front of him, slim but curved in all the right places and barely reaching up to his chin, Emma looked like a terrier ready to take on a rottweiler. Her workout clothes were rumpled from sitting on the grass, and her skin glowed with recent exertion. Her hair was carelessly twisted at the back and caught up in a tortoiseshell clip, making him want to undo the golden mass and send it tumbling to her shoulders. The red-gold strands curling around her ears and nape teased at him like a promise of things to come.

He pushed the thought away. Somehow she'd gotten the idea that he wanted more from her than her catering skills. Unfortunately, she wasn't entirely wrong. He'd felt the attraction between them from first meeting. He'd seen her brother slip the vodka into her drink, but hadn't known until later that it wasn't her idea, intrigued to think she needed Dutch courage to approach him.

Since then he'd relived the memory of her kiss more times than was good for him. Her approach had been naive, fueled by the party mood, but the taste of her had awakened a desire for more. When Cherie had suggested he talk to Emma about his birthday dinner, he'd felt like a nervous teenager.

Unlike the model types he usually dated, Emma wasn't beautiful in the runway sense. Her looks were too distinctive, her nose a fraction too sharp, and her mouth a touch wide for perfection. But when she smiled or gave her infectious laugh, she was stunning. A pang of jealousy still gripped him when he thought of her laughing with another man at her parents' function. She hadn't ever laughed with Nate like that.

Her sea-green eyes shone now and she clasped her hands together, her expression daring him not to take her seriously. "You'd better explain what you mean, because I seem to have missed a step or two."

"I doubt you've missed a step in your life, *Dr. Hale*," she said. "Did my mother suggest I might be part of the package if you hired me?"

His patience was becoming strained. "I can't deny it's an attractive thought. But if anyone put that idea in my head, it was you."

She looked taken aback. He was almost sorry to see some of the fire fade from her eyes. Anger was a pure, honest emotion, stripping a person of artifice. What you saw was what you got. And in Emma's case, what he saw was enough to raise his blood pressure several points.

"Really?" She sounded skeptical. "We've had only one business meeting."

"And another meeting that was pure pleasure." For him, anyway. It was hardly his fault if she felt embarrassed by the encounter. He'd go back for seconds anytime.

Color bloomed in her cheeks. "I might have known you'd bring that up. I made one mistake…"

"Are you sure it was a mistake?"

"It—it had to be. I didn't want…"

Her stammered denial was enough to convince him that she'd been as affected by their brief kiss as he had. He was tempted to see if the chemistry he recalled was still potent and leaned close enough to feel her breath whispering across his mouth before he caught himself. His shoulders felt stiff as he pulled back, and a growing discomfort told him they weren't the only part of him hardening. He was going to end up proving her right about scheming to have her as part of the package.

"You have some rigid ideas about doctors' lives," he said. "I invited you along on this walk to show you we aren't all the same. If you and I are going to work together, it will be easier if you stop treating me as the enemy. You can't deny that's what you've been doing."

She let her hands drop to her sides. "Any ideas I have are based on long experience."

"Not with me."

"No."

But her tone said she reserved the right to toss him in with all the other medical people she knew. What had they done to her to prejudice her so thoroughly against an entire profession? Most people thought of doctors as valuable members of a community. Emma treated them as arrogant bastards who were out to make her life unpleasant. Maybe while she worked for him, he could ferret out the reasons for her hostility. He realized he wanted to do that very much. Did he think that once he overcame the hurdle, whatever it was, he'd have a chance to get to first base with her? That seemed selfish. Yet the more he tried to convince himself he wanted to help for Emma's sake only, the hollower it sounded.

His own psychoanalysis could wait, he decided. There was still that blasted party he didn't want, but which his friends clearly expected him to make happen. He found he also didn't want to do it without Emma. Afterward, he could worry about where they went next.

EMMA'S THOUGHTS WERE IN turmoil as they set off again down the wide path past Timbrell Park, where a family group was enjoying a ball game. Seeing a father chase after his toddler, she felt an unexpected pang. What would it be like to have a man give you children, then cherish you both the way this man obviously did?

The child giggled as he was scooped up and carried shoulder-high back to his mother. The sight made Emma smile. What a contrast to her own father, rigid with anger, returning his four-year-old Emma to her mother in Gramma Jessie's kitchen.

Emma's smile faded. No loving warmth for her, only disapproval over the worry she'd caused. Emma's cuts and scrapes had been treated with clinical care, but her emotional distress had been completely ignored. As an adult, she still suffered occasional nightmares about being lost in a dark, forbidding place as a result of that experience, but apart from Jessie's interest, her family had never mentioned the incident again.

She dismissed the memory and focused on Nate's assertion that she was the one putting ideas into his head. One impetuous kiss at a party didn't amount to an open invitation. Had she sent subtle signals of her interest to him in other ways she hadn't been aware of, or was he simply confirming her belief that doctors made their own rules?

The solution was to be as clinical as her parents in her dealings with Nate. From now on there would be no casual meetings in gardens, on walking trails or anywhere outside their respective offices. He would soon get the message that their dealings were to be strictly business.

Nate looked equally deep in thought as they paced out the remaining distance back to the Iron Cove

Bridge. She'd read that the bridge had replaced an earlier one from the eighteen-eighties that had once carried trams, and tried to imagine the now busy suburbs when horses and carts had ruled the roads.

She wouldn't have minded living in those times, when the pace of life was slower, although she knew she'd miss her work. Cooking had been less of a leisure activity then and done for simple sustenance, with less varied ingredients than she was used to. A party like Nate's would have been a rowdy affair rather than the nostalgia trip she had in mind.

Realizing she was making a bad habit of picturing him in domestic scenes, she forced her mind back to the plans she wanted to discuss with him. The written proposal with detailed costings had been sent by cab, but he wouldn't have had time to go over them yet. They were nearly at the end of the walk and she wondered if he intended to have a business meeting at the rowing club overlooking Iron Cove Bay. With the sun splashing golden light across the darkening sky, she would have to work to keep her mind on the job.

But he walked past the club, stopping in front of a small café she hadn't noticed when they set off. The Flying Fox Café was lettered across the front of what had been a worker's cottage in the time of the old bridge and the trams. Now the charmingly restored building opened onto a deck with a view of the bay. A rustling sound in the thick greenery beside

the cottage drew her eye upward to a group of flying
foxes preparing to set off in search of their night's
meal, making it obvious where the café got its name.
She smiled, enjoying the presence of wildlife so close
to the city.

"Hungry?" Nate asked over his shoulder as he
strode toward the cottage.

"A little," she admitted.

"You'll like this place," he said, leading her through
the front door into a modern eatery with polished wood
floors and pale wood and chrome furniture. The tables
were far enough apart for privacy, and concertina glass
doors opened the opposite wall to the view beyond.
"You and Angie Fox should be on the same wavelength.
She's an amazing cook."

Did Nate think of Emma in that way? Good, it
should help her professionally, she thought, pushing away an unwelcome rush of gratification. An
attractive blonde woman straightened from behind
the counter where she'd been arranging exquisitely
decorated cupcakes. "Nate," she said warmly. "You
must have radar. Today's special is your favorite,
gazpacho."

"Angie Fox, this is Emma Jarrett. Food is her specialty, too."

Emma saw questions in the other woman's eyes
as they exchanged greetings. Either Emma was the
latest of many females Nate had brought here and
Angie wanted to know more, or the situation was

novel enough to make her curious. While Emma suspected it wasn't the latter, she didn't want to suggest a personal interest in him, so she avoided saying anything. Instead, she chatted to Angie about her work, leaving a card when the other woman wanted to know if she supplied small businesses. She hadn't so far, but it didn't mean she couldn't.

Angie waved toward the deck where early diners were already seated. "I'll bring your food over. Outside or in here?"

She didn't ask what Emma wanted to eat and neither did Nate. "In here is fine. We have some business to discuss."

She should welcome the reminder of why she was here, Emma told herself. The deck was too romantic for a business meeting, although her whole body vibrated with an energy that had nothing to do with work.

Emma felt Nate's probing amber eyes looking at her from under long, silky lashes as she seated herself across from him.

A squeal and the sound of running feet short-circuited Emma's thoughts as a little girl of three or four came racing up, a picture book clutched in her hands. "Dr. Nate." Seeing the stranger with him, the child stopped short, tucking herself close to Nate for reassurance.

He wrapped an arm around her in a hug. "Natalie, this is my friend, Emma."

Emma smiled. "Hello, Natalie. What are you reading?"

"I can't read, but I like dinosaurs," the child said. She shoved the book toward Nate. "Mummy says this is a terry duck tail."

The well-worn book was open at a colorful cartoon of a pterodactyl, Emma noticed, suppressing a grin. *Terry duck tail* was close enough. Nate thought so, too, because he let the child ramble on, seeming in no hurry to be rid of her. The sight of his cropped dark hair close to Natalie's blond curls as he gave her his full attention made Emma's stomach knot. She switched her attention to the cell phone he'd placed on the table when they sat down. That was reality. Even the child recognized him as "Dr. Nate." Emma should do the same.

Angie came to the table carrying a tray with brimming bowls of chilled soup and side plates of grilled, marinated prawn sticks. The aroma of herbs and garlic excited Emma's already heightened senses. Glasses were on the table and Angie placed a carafe of water with lemon slices next to them. She turned to the child. "Take your book back to your room and let Dr. Nate have his dinner." To Nate, she added, "Let me know when you're ready for coffee."

Emma caught the faintest hint of an accent. Swedish? She looked at the woman curiously as she shepherded the child away. "Angie is talented," she said, casting a professional eye over the skilled presentation of their food.

He nodded. "One of the best."

Emma wanted to ask why he hadn't invited someone who was evidently a close friend to cater his party, but he anticipated the question. "Angie was a patient. She was pregnant with Natalie when she needed urgent heart surgery."

"You managed to save both of them." Emma was annoyed to feel relieved as his relationship with the other woman became clear. Another thought occurred to her. "Is Natalie…"

"Named for me," he said, his voice gruff. "Angie wouldn't be talked out of it. I tell her she works too hard, but she loves this place and she only opens the hours she can manage and still look after Natalie."

Was he this close to all his former patients? Emma wondered as she bit into one of the prawn skewers. A delicious blend of seafood and herbs filled her mouth. When she tried the soup, it turned out to be the white version of gazpacho called *ajo blanco*. Judging by the silky texture, Angie had soaked the blanched almonds in milk before processing them with bread, seedless green grapes and garlic, olive oil, vinegar and seasonings. Delicious.

Emma hadn't been aware of closing her eyes until she opened them to find Nate watching her, an amused expression on his face. "Good, isn't it?"

"Blissful. I'd love to get her recipe."

"You're in luck. I have some pull with the owner."

She fell silent, relishing the tastes and textures of the simple, well-prepared food. Sometimes she got annoyed when she couldn't stop herself from deconstructing the taste of a particular dish. This time, so many of her senses were engaged that it was easy to let herself go and simply enjoy the experience. Being with Nate was like that, came the unbidden thought. He swamped her senses until she had trouble working out what was going on.

The evening was warm but she shivered. Professional, she reminded herself. Businesslike. Amazing how hard she found it to force her thoughts into that mode. Swallowing the last creamy mouthful of *ajo blanco,* she rested the spoon in the bowl. "We should talk about your event, although I don't know what I can tell you until you've gone over my suggestions."

Angie came over and took their coffee orders, flatly refusing to let him pay for the meal. Emma suspected it was a ritual played out whenever Nate came here, and envied the warmth between them as they sparred.

When Angie left them alone, he leaned forward. "Never mind the details. I can read them when I get home. Talk me through how you see the night unfolding."

He meant the party night, she reminded herself, but visions of where they might go after dinner ran riot through her mind.

NATE WATCHED HER, HIS THOUGHTS racing. Normally he did the bay walk with half his mind still back at the hospital. Tonight, his patients had barely entered his mind. It was true, his assistant was competent. Nate had trained Grace Lockwood himself. And she was backed by a team he'd also handpicked. Still, finding himself totally in the moment, as he'd been with Emma tonight, was unusual enough to make him wonder what was going on.

"I did some research into your life," she began.

Instantly he felt his hackles rise. "My life story isn't your concern."

"Everything about my client is my concern," she countered. "I can't tailor an event to suit someone I don't know."

"Point taken." All the same, it bothered him. He wasn't ashamed of his background but it didn't fill him with pride, either. Warring parents and a rebel half brother were hardly the Brady Bunch. "I can't imagine you learned anything useful from what's on record."

She stirred her coffee, looking thoughtful. "You'd be surprised. For instance, I suspect you never had much of a family life."

Only his training kept the surprise off his face.

"My father's the backbone of his town, and my mother's been with my stepdad for more than twenty years. Isn't that stable enough for you?"

She met his gaze unflinchingly. "In my experience, pillars of the community don't have a lot of time for their own families."

Poker-faced, he swallowed a mouthful of coffee. She'd started this, let her finish it. "Go on."

"Busy professional parents often don't make time to cook and eat with their kids."

"True." He hated the admission, but damn it, she was right. Growing up, he'd spent more time eating with his friends' families than with his own. Later, medical texts had been his main dinner companions.

"If you're used to eating out all the time and exploring exotic foods, where's the novelty in doing more of the same?"

"You tell me."

Warming to her topic, she went on. "I want to hire a bunch of large old-style tables, dress them as family settings and serve the kind of comfort food we associate with growing up, like sausages and mash."

A feeling he recognized as resistance strummed through him. He didn't want reminders of what he'd never had. He scrubbed his hand down his face, trying to chase away the discomfort. Emma didn't need to feel sorry for him, or know as much about him as she evidently did. He felt exposed, and lashed out instinctively.

"Is this a dinner or a therapy session?" Taking his anger out on her wasn't fair, but he didn't feel fair right now. Because she was getting too close to home? He shoved that thought away, too.

"It's a party," she said.

Her tone didn't change but he saw her eyes cloud with hurt, making him feel brutal. He wanted to take back his words and kiss away the self-doubt he'd sown.

Instead, Nate played devil's advocate. "Do you seriously mean to serve my guests sausages and mash?"

"Yes, except the sausage will be *saucisse de Toulouse,* the homemade sausage you find in a French cassoulet," she pointed out, "served the way our mothers would have done if they'd had a clue."

"Just because you had problems with your parents doesn't mean everyone does," he said, annoyed at sounding so defensive.

"I only said that they were busy with careers and demands outside their homes. I'll bet many of your guests' childhoods were the same. They'll get the biggest kick out of this experience. And if their families were close, it will be a nostalgia trip."

He drained his coffee. "Personally, I think nostalgia is overrated."

ON THE TABLE BETWEEN THEM, Nate's phone jumped, startling them both. When he flipped it open, Emma told herself she'd been lucky to have his undivided attention for this long.

He didn't like her idea for his party. No, he resisted her idea, she amended the thought. His childhood had mirrored her own, she'd swear to it. His hurt probably ran every bit as deep. But being a man, he'd made a virtue of toughness, refusing to admit his feelings to anyone, perhaps not even to himself.

Should she offer him another option that wouldn't push so many buttons? It was her job to give her clients wonderful food and a memorable event, not to fix whatever troubled them. It also wasn't her job to socialize with them, but she'd done it tonight. And sat with him in his favorite café while the sun set around them. And wished he was with her because he wanted to be.

Get a grip, she instructed herself. Nate was already so focused on his call, he'd forgotten she existed. So what if he was disappointed with her? She hadn't wanted to work with him from the start. Being around such a physically attractive man had distracted her from reality, that was all. Their priorities were still light-years apart.

With the truth staring her in the face, she stood up then remembered she had no money with her for a cab, and her only way home was in Nate's car.

He lifted a hand, gesturing for her to wait.

Resentment flared until she saw the look on his face. Instead of calm, medical competence, she read something like fear.

She sat down again and linked her hands on the table. His side of the conversation suggested something was wrong, but she didn't know him well enough to put the pieces together. When he closed the phone, his look was shuttered. "I'll call a cab to get you home."

"I don't have…"

He got to his feet. "I know. This should cover the fare."

She had no choice but to accept the notes he held out, although the dismissal rankled. "Can I do anything to help?"

"See yourself home."

As if she hadn't already worked that out. "I mean with whatever's happened."

His arctic look raked her. "For what it's worth, you were right when you said my family life wasn't up to much. The proof is my messed-up half brother, Luke. He's taken off in my mother's car."

"You think he might come to you?"

"If we're lucky. If not, he's risking his neck with the tough kids he hangs out with when he should be at school."

Her breath escaped in a rush. "I had no idea, Nate, or I wouldn't have forced my scheme on you."

His hands skimmed her shoulders, the touch fiery.

"You didn't. I have to help find Luke, but I'll go over your proposal as soon as I can and be in touch."

"Thanks." No way would he accept her ideas after this. She felt foolishly disappointed.

When the cab arrived, Nate hurriedly helped her into it, and Emma struggled not to feel bitter. She didn't expect him to choose between her and his brother. The truth was she wanted to stay and help him, not be sent away. "Let me know if there's anything I can do," she said, wishing she had more to offer.

"Sure." He closed the door. But instead of heading for his car, he waited while the cab pulled away, cutting a solitary figure in the light spilling from the Flying Fox Café.

A powerful urge to have the driver turn around and take her back to Nate made Emma catch her breath. There was nothing she could do. She'd be in his way. Leaving him alone was the only sensible option. At the same time, it didn't seem right.

## CHAPTER FIVE

AN ODD EMPTINESS WRENCHED AT Nate as he watched Emma's cab accelerate out of sight. He should be with her, not heading off on another wild-goose chase to bail out his brother.

Nate had been twenty when Luke was born. Rather than develop in his own time, Luke had wanted to keep up with Nate. Trying to compete at sports when sheer size gave Nate the advantage was the least of Luke's problems. At twelve, he'd linked up with a street gang, drinking and acting tough, thinking he'd found a shortcut to manhood.

In sight of the Branxton, Nate pressed the remote and was soon pulling out into the traffic with only a rough idea of where to start looking. His mother and stepfather had to take some of the blame, he knew. His half brother's life had been very different from Nate's. More time, money and attention were lavished on the younger boy, for all the good it did him.

Instead of coming down hard the first time Luke went off the rails, his parents had tried counseling, and when that failed, bribery. But they'd only increased Luke's sense of entitlement, and he became more headstrong and out of control.

Now he was fifteen with a boy's mind in a man's body and friends who gave Nate the shivers when he had to be around them. Mostly veterans of jails and halfway houses in their teens, they cared for nothing and nobody but themselves.

Nate felt his mouth thin. Was it any wonder he'd resisted Emma's vision of a nostalgic family dinner for his birthday? She hadn't been in his shoes, trying to keep his medical studies together while the family lurched from one Luke-driven drama to another.

The kid didn't know how well off he was, Nate thought, gripping the steering wheel hard enough to turn his knuckles white. When Luke was born, both parents were there for him. His father came home on time most evenings. As a lawyer, Josh hadn't been on call at all hours and there was always money for whatever Luke wanted to do.

Focus, Nate told himself. What mattered now was finding the kid and their mother's car before anybody got hurt. A call to Joanna told him Luke hadn't shown up at his own house. He knew the gang's inner-city territory and headed there, scanning the side streets for the blue Audi his stepfather had given his mother on her last birthday.

There was no sign of the car near the boarded-up mechanic's workshop the gang used as their headquarters, or at any of their usual haunts. If Luke was out joyriding, this could take all night.

But luck was with Nate. A few blocks further on he spotted the car parked across from a convenience store, and went cold. Luke was in the front passenger seat, two friends with him, all watching the store. It didn't take a genius to figure out what they had in mind. Well, not if Nate could help it. He eased the Branxton into the space in front of the Audi, almost touching bumpers. Then he leaned on the horn.

At the noise, lights popped on and a few choice phrases were hurled from upstairs windows, telling him where to stick the horn. A tall, thin man appeared at the front of the store carrying a baseball bat in one hand and a cell phone in the other.

Nate wound down his window as Luke appeared in the opening, his expression wild.

"What the hell you doing here, man?" he demanded.

"Saving you from yourself. Get in."

"Piss off. I'm not a kid you can drag home. I have things to do tonight."

Releasing the horn, Nate gestured toward the man with the baseball bat, the cell phone now pressed to his ear. "I can guess what kind of things. Your target looks like he's calling the cops. If you don't want to be here when they arrive, I suggest you get in. Now."

Luke seemed confused, for a moment looking his

true age. "Man, this sucks. I'll never be able to face the guys after this."

"That's the general idea." Nate unlocked the passenger door. In the rearview mirror, he saw Luke's would-be accomplices abandon the Audi and slink off down an alley, also making themselves scarce before things heated up. Luke's fists crashed against the Branxton's roof and Nate winced, bracing himself for the stream of crude language that followed. "Feel better now?" he asked mildly.

Luke spat out some more phrases but slammed around to the passenger side and got in, slumping as far away from Nate as he could.

Nate got out, retrieved the keys and locked the Audi. No actual crime had been committed, so the cops couldn't charge Luke with anything, although they could trace the car to his mother. When he returned, Luke hadn't moved, but fastened his seat belt at Nate's command and stayed sullenly silent on the drive home.

Judging by his stepfather's white-faced anger as he heard the story, Nate guessed Luke was in for a rough time. But it was rougher than Nate expected. "Josh is trying to arrange for Luke to spend some time behind bars as part of a program to head off criminal behavior," his mother told him when father and son were out of earshot.

Being gentle with Luke sure hadn't worked, Nate thought. He'd heard about such programs, and as a lawyer, his stepfather had the right connections. "Tough love is sometimes the only solution," he said.

He saw his mother's eyes brim. "I wanted us to be a happy family. By leaving your father, I only caused a new set of problems, didn't I?"

Nate patted her shoulder. "You did what you thought was right at the time. Luke's a good kid at heart. He just needs to know the world doesn't exist for his benefit."

"You never thought it did. Why can't he be more like you, helping people instead of hurting them?"

"Trying to be like me is half his problem," Nate insisted. "I'll always have a twenty-year head start. Luke needs to find out who he is, and what he can become. It might help if you stop comparing us so much."

She nodded. "You're right, and I'll try. Thanks for getting him out of trouble tonight. If those other boys had ganged up on you instead of running away…"

The same thought had occurred to Nate. "They didn't." He leaned down to kiss her on the cheek. "I'd better get home. It's been a long day."

"Were you at work when Josh called you?"

Nate felt his face heat. "I was having dinner with a business associate."

She read the truth in his heightened color. "I hope she's nice."

She is, thought Nate as he left the house without

enlightening his mother any further. Emma was much too nice for the way he'd treated her tonight. Luke's need for a sense of belonging and his mother's wish for a happy family suggested Emma's idea had merit. Maybe Brady Bunch families were pie-in-the-sky, but could it hurt to enjoy the fantasy for one night?

Emma was also dangerous, he thought as he drove home. She planted ideas in his head he could do without, like sitting at a large table, a woman beside him, and a bunch of kids of different ages around them. How many times had *that* been reality, even just the three of them, when his mother was still married to his father? Now his family was in an uproar over Luke. And Emma herself had grown up with absentee parents. No fantasies for any of them.

By the time Nate got home, fatigue was setting in like a drug. Joanna had left Emma's envelope on the hall table with the rest of his mail. He resisted the urge to pick it up simply because it came from her, and headed to the shower.

Half an hour later, barefoot and clad only in sleep shorts, he walked into the living room carrying the envelope but placed it on the coffee table. He was too wired to relax and would never make sense of anything he read. Emma deserved better.

Thoughts of her jumbled with the difficult case he'd handled earlier today. Twice his patient had died on the table, and twice they'd brought the man back from the edge in a stressful nine hours of surgery.

No wonder Nate had needed to burn off tension with physical exertion. Inviting Emma along had been a practical use of time. It had nothing to do with the fact he felt refreshed being with her.

He stopped pacing and ran his palms over his damp hair. He'd hated sending her away, but needed to know she was safe. Nate's blood chilled as he thought of what could have happened if Luke's friends had taken him on. Not long ago, he'd caught Luke sharpening a large screwdriver, the gang's weapon of choice. If the night had turned out differently, Nate could have ended up on his own operating table. Risking his safety was one thing, but he hadn't been about to risk hers.

He hoped Luke had learned something tonight, or would after the day behind bars his father had planned for him. Tough love, Nate thought. Was there any other kind?

He poured a stiff Scotch, but let it sit beside Emma's envelope as he threw himself onto his favorite leather chaise, one of the few pieces of furniture the decorator had recommended that accommodated his long legs. He couldn't remember when he'd felt more tired or less ready for sleep.

With a sigh he reached for the envelope. As he flipped through the folder, he was impressed by the pains she'd taken, not only in planning the menu, but in suggesting how the event should be stage-managed to best effect.

He'd barely started reading when the print blurred before his eyes. Massaging his temples didn't help. He became aware of how silent the house was. Joanna preferred not to live in, and had left for the night. Normally, Nate enjoyed the quiet, but tonight he felt lonely. He tried not to picture Emma curled at the other end of the couch, and was irritated at how easily her image filled his mind. No way would he see her there in his lifetime.

With good reason. He remembered only too well the many nights his mother had sat up waiting for his father, while dinner shriveled along with the love his parents had once shared. The memory was still in Nate's mind as he drifted off, the folder open on his knees and the drink untouched.

EMMA'S THOUGHTS WERE in overdrive. She'd changed into lounging pajamas and was stretched out on the sofa with a mug of chamomile tea, trying to unwind enough for bed. Shopping at the markets for fresh ingredients for the bowlers' club lunch felt like days ago instead of first thing this morning. Between helping prep the food, and working up the proposal for Nate, she'd put in a full day, and that was before doing his seven-kilometer walk.

Not that she'd done herself much good. He'd invited her along for his convenience, not because he wanted her company. It wasn't—couldn't be— personal. Her mother thought he was ideal husband material, but like all the medical types Emma knew, Nate was already married to his work. All the same, his rejection of her family-dinner concept had singed her pride.

But he cared enough about his half brother to go off into the night to find him. She sipped her tea. His anguish had been genuine, and for Luke rather than himself. The contrast between Nate's concern and her father's coldness the day she got lost in the bush was impossible to ignore.

She glanced at the Marilyn Monroe clock on the wall, the movie legend's white skirt forever billowing as time marched past her. It was midnight but Emma wouldn't sleep until she knew what had happened with Luke. Until she knew Nate was safe. She chased that thought away and picked up the phone.

Several rings later, she was about to hang up when he answered, "Hale speaking."

She recognized his surgeon's voice. He probably thought someone from the hospital was calling. "It's Emma," she said quickly. "I hope I didn't wake you up."

"I was reading your proposal. I didn't realize I'd dozed off."

*Flattery will get you everywhere,* she thought, miffed that her work had managed to put him to sleep. "I gather the crisis with Luke is over." She had trouble keeping the hurt out of her voice. "I'll call back another time."

"It's okay, I'm awake now."

She imagined him rubbing his chin between thumb and forefinger in a gesture she already knew was characteristic. "I only wanted to see if you found Luke." And to know you were okay.

"Yeah, I found him." He paused and she heard ice clink in a glass. "Luckily before he and two of his gang robbed a convenience store."

"You didn't try to stop them on your own!" Three against one. Her breath snagged. This time she couldn't hold back the reaction. "Oh, my God, are you all right?"

"Worried about me, Emma?" The surgeon's crisp voice slid into a huskier, more intimate tone.

The picture of him fighting off a gang of hulking teenagers was vivid and disturbing. She took refuge in anger. "Of course I was. Why didn't you call the police?"

"If I'd known what to tell them, I would have. But until I saw Luke and his mates casing the store, I was flying blind."

Her breathing shallowed. "Then I suppose you waded in with fists flying."

The ice clinked again and she heard him swallow. "I wasn't risking my hands. I simply made enough noise to ruin their plan. Luke came over to my car to ream me out, and his fine friends couldn't get out of there fast enough."

The gang could still have turned on him. She

imagined Nate sprawled on the road, hurt or worse. "What about your brother?"

"Luke's okay, too. After tonight, he hates my guts, but I can live with that as long as he stays out of trouble. My stepfather intends to make sure he does."

Tears blurred her vision. Todd's air of superiority might rankle because he was the doctor, but her brother had never given their family such grief. "I hope it works," she said.

"Makes two of us," Nate agreed. "After all the drama, I need something else in my head. Tell me what you're doing at this moment."

"Besides calling you?" she asked, feeling her face heat. Why hadn't she texted him instead of getting herself into this?

"Yep. Start with what you're wearing."

Shock made her blurt out the truth. "Coffee-colored lounging pajamas."

"Nothing else?"

Her stomach knotted. "Nate!"

His laughter vibrated down the line. "You're blushing, I can tell."

"I am not."

"Yes, you are."

She pulled her legs close to her body in an unconsciously defensive posture. "All right then, two can play. What are you wearing?"

"Sleep shorts with red devils on them." He sounded far more relaxed than she was.

"Seems appropriate."

"You think of me as a devil?"

"Only when you act like one. Like you're doing now."

"Have you thought you might bring out the devil in me?" His voice was low and sexy.

She'd had enough, not only of his dismissal of her work, but the way her body temperature insisted on soaring at the sound of his voice. "You must be mixing me up with the other Emma," she said tartly.

"WHAT OTHER EMMA?" NATE searched his memory but came up blank.

"On the phone when I reminded you about our meeting, you mentioned another Emma you thought you had a date with tonight."

"Oh, her. My mind was on other things." Like the touch-and-go outcome of a nine-hour surgery, he recalled.

"I'm sure she'd be flattered."

Emma actually sounded angry, and Nate felt a stirring of regret. She was so easy to tease that he'd forgotten women liked to think they were the only one in a man's life. Not that she was. They were merely business associates, as he'd told his mother. Still, he didn't like hurting her feelings. "The other

Emma, as you call her, is a family friend from Tasmania. When she moved to Sydney last November, I took her out a few times to help her find her feet in the big city. Happy now?"

"It's hardly any of my concern. I'm more worried that we didn't make progress on planning your event."

Nate picked up the relief in her voice and wasn't sure he believed her.

"What kind of progress should we make?"

"You know I mean with your event." Her voice had an edge to it. "Though if my proposal put you to sleep, that may be an answer in itself."

Nate's conscience twinged as he looked at the pages scattered around the chaise. "I'd barely started reading when I nodded off."

"Better and better."

Hearing the censure in her voice, he felt something snap inside. He'd looked forward to telling her he was warming to her idea of a family-themed party. Instead, he let stress and exhaustion speak for him. "Look, whatever you decide is fine with me. Why don't you go ahead and make it happen?"

"You don't want to be consulted?"

"You and Joanna can work out most of what you need between you, as long as you keep me informed."

"Naturally I will," she said coolly.

He'd added insult to injury, but he was hiring her,

for pity's sake. He should have kept this professional instead of triggering feelings he'd rather not have to deal with.

A picture formed in his mind of her gorgeous sun-kissed hair held by one of those clip things. Was it down now, loose and flowing over—what was it she'd said she was wearing?—lounging pajamas? He didn't know exactly what they were, but imagined filmy harem pants and a strappy top outlining her slender curves. Pajamas suggested bed. He felt the red devils stirring to life around his groin, and slammed a lid on any thoughts of bed and Emma together.

Between the sudden awakening from REM sleep and the Scotch, which was now half-gone, he wasn't thinking straight. He could still tell when he'd done damage, and his sense of decency made him say, "You know your business, Emma. I don't need detailed reports."

"What you need is a demonstration."

The red devils went crazy. "What?"

"It's time you rediscovered home cooking and got a feel for what I want to do for you. I'll cook some of the dishes myself at your place this Friday night if you're available."

"Friday's open, but why cook in my kitchen?"

"I'll be working there on the night of your party. Call it a road test."

Having her in his house hovered dangerously close

to his fantasy, but he couldn't tell her why everything in him wanted to turn her down. "Friday it is then."

As soon as the words left his mouth, second thoughts assailed him. In trying to soothe her ruffled feelings, he'd committed himself when he couldn't guarantee to follow through. All it took was another close call in surgery, and all bets were off. But the mistake was made.

"I'll be there when you get home," she agreed. "In the meantime, you might finish reading my proposal when you're awake."

She was like a terrier with a bone, he thought. But she was right about this. "I'll read it first thing tomorrow. But only as a formality. You can consider yourself hired as of tonight. The budget is no object, so spend whatever you think appropriate. Email me how much you need as a deposit, and I'll have the money transferred to your business account ASAP."

SHE SHOULD FEEL PLEASED, Emma thought as she thanked him and hung up the phone. Instead, she felt unsettled.

Her tea had cooled, so she went to the kitchen to make a fresh cup. While she waited for the water to boil, a vision of Nate in shorts, chest bare, rose in her mind. Heat spread through her, molten and wild, and her breath caught. What was going on here?

Why on earth had she suggested cooking dinner for him? He'd been ready to leave everything to her, which should have been enough. If he hadn't confessed to falling asleep while reading her proposal, she'd never have offered a demonstration.

Exactly what was she trying to prove? An image of awakening a sleeping tiger came to mind, and was just as quickly banished. He was an attractive man, but a doctor to his bootstraps. Always busy, always with a good excuse for running late. Never time or attention for anything but his work. She'd be lucky if he showed at all on Friday.

On the other hand, being stood up might convince her how crazy she'd be to let herself think of Nate as anything but a client. Having her carefully prepared meal go to waste might help her shake off this insane preoccupation. The way her body hummed like a tuning fork and her hand wavered as she poured water over the chamomile leaves made the prospect unlikely. She'd never felt this alive thinking about a man. And she didn't want to now, especially not over Nate.

Tea in hand, she paused at the kitchen door, her hand on the light switch. Life would be a lot simpler if feelings also came with an off switch, she thought as she darkened the room and headed for bed.

## CHAPTER SIX

NATE MADE SURE HE WAS ON TIME on Friday. Citing the need to tackle a backlog of paperwork, which was true, he'd scheduled his last operation for early in the day, and had time to check on his recovering patients and make inroads into the tower of files on his desk before leaning back in his chair and stretching.

Grace Lockwood, his assistant and a brilliant surgeon in her own right, came into his office and added another file to the tower, ignoring his grimace. "How's the party plan coming along?"

"I'm road testing some of the food tonight."

"Personal service. I'm impressed. Cherie Kenner-Jarrett's daughter is your caterer, isn't she?" When he nodded, Grace said, "Let me know how the road test goes. I have friends who want help with their son's eighteenth."

"Oh, to be eighteen again."

"Trust me, you don't want to go there. My eldest turns eighteen this year, too. The drive-by hormone attacks are scary."

Thinking of Luke, Nate was inclined to agree. "You've never regretted having kids?"

"On the hour, every hour. Wouldn't swap them for the world."

"What about juggling family life with all this?" He waved toward the files.

She didn't hesitate. "If it comes to a choice, family wins every time. Otherwise, Mike and I wouldn't have lasted this long."

"My father never got the balance right."

Grace regarded him keenly. "It's in the willingness, not the genes, Nate, in case you decide to take the plunge."

He affected a shudder. "I'm already married to this place."

"Here's another morsel of wisdom for you. Never love anything that can't love you back." Her pager beeped and she checked it. "Duty calls. Have fun with your paperwork."

Some fun, he thought, surprised by a rush of resentment. A surgeon was all he'd ever wanted to be. Suddenly everyone was chipping away at the foundations of his life. He admired and respected Grace, but putting personal life ahead of work wasn't always possible. How could you turn your back on someone whose life depended on you?

He thought of his mother. Her emotional life had depended on her husband, and she'd been let down more times than she could tolerate. The marriage had eventually died.

Nate swore under his breath. Why did it come

down to a choice? People who married doctors had to know what they were getting into. If they couldn't stand the heat, they shouldn't be in the kitchen.

And thinking of kitchens, Emma would be in his house by now. No way would he add to her low opinion of doctors by getting home late. Refusing to wonder why her opinion mattered to him, he hung up his white coat and left the hospital. The startled looks he got as he walked out on time irritated him by suggesting that Emma had a point.

By the time he pulled into his garage, he'd worked up a first-class appetite. For food, he told himself. Only for food. Inside, he was greeted by aromas he hadn't known his kitchen could produce. He bit back the urge to call out, "Honey, I'm home." Emma was a paid professional.

Her appearance at the kitchen door, wiping her hands on an apron, didn't help. "Nate, you're on time."

"Don't sound so surprised."

"And cranky, too."

The effort not to move closer was agonizing. "I'm not cranky, damn it."

"Evidently not."

She turned back into the kitchen and he followed her, determined not to be thrown by the unaccustomed domesticity. And stopped in his tracks when he saw the chaos. Pots and pans were piled high. The mirror glass oven doors were fogged, and dishes revolved in the microwave. "Bet you've never seen your kitchen like this," she said.

"All this for one meal?"

"I made a few extras, cookies and squares to fill those gorgeous Villeroy & Boch containers that look like they've never been used. You're getting the whole home-cooking experience."

She held out a jar and he looked inside. Huge chocolate cookies glistened, and he couldn't resist. He dipped, lifted, bit and went to heaven.

"Hey, those are for later."

"Never mind dinner, I'll just have these."

She wrestled the jar away. "Shower. Change. Dinner's in thirty minutes."

He should object to being ordered around in his own home, but instead he felt cared for. Emma had chocolate on her cheek. He reached out a crooked finger and erased the smudge, hearing her suck in a breath. "Shower," she said, sounding husky.

He didn't trust himself to linger.

EMMA'S FACE FELT FLUSHED from more than the cooking. The touch of Nate's finger, like a butterfly wing on her cheek, had speared through her. He'd looked as if he wanted to do more, and heaven help her, so did she.

A timer pinged a welcome distraction. By the time Nate's thirty minutes were up, she had herself back under control. Joanna had set the table before going home so Emma only needed to serve the courses and wait for Nate's reaction.

When she went into the dining room, he was staring at the table and frowning. "Set another place. You're joining me."

"Nate, I shouldn't…"

"Either we eat together or the whole meal is wasted."

He didn't leave her much choice. Flustered, she added another place setting but he didn't sit down until she carried in the first course and he pulled out a chair for her.

Across from her, he studied the first dish. "Fish cakes?"

"I promised you home cooking."

He forked a bite into his mouth and a blissful expression took hold. "This is like no fish cake I've ever tasted."

She sampled her own. "Because you've never had them made with Tasmanian salmon, anchovy essence and my special coating of Italian breadcrumbs and polenta. Try adding some of the lime dressing."

He did and rolled his eyes. "I thought the cookies were sublime."

She basked in his enthusiasm. Purely out of professional pride. "Wait till you taste the rest."

He gave her an assessing look. "I can hardly wait."

Glad of the excuse to escape to the kitchen, she

sipped water to steady herself before plating up her secret weapon—meat loaf. The aroma from the mushrooms, mozzarella and herbs rolled in a layer of spiced ground beef and veal was perfect. She arranged the slices on beds of baby field greens and mounded truffled mashed potatoes beside them.

When she served Nate, he inhaled curiously. "What's this?"

"Meat loaf."

He took a bite, chewed slowly, swallowed then actually moaned. "No it's not, it's an orgasm on a plate."

Emma wasn't sure how to respond to that. "This is what I want your guests to experience. I mean—the best of home cooking, not…um…"

"An orgasm?" His gaze sparkled. "You've certainly convinced me." He finished the dish in silence, which to Emma was a greater compliment than words.

Her final course of *baba au rhum* with almond praline ice cream also got his seal of approval. But when she reached to remove his plate, he grasped her hand. "I'll do that. You've earned a break."

"It's my job."

He stood up, not exactly towering over her, but still making it clear he would have his way. "You've done your job. And proved your point."

She wasn't sure how she got from wrestling over a plate to being held against the hard wall of his chest.

She'd always known sharing food could be bonding, but this?

His breath was fragrant with the rum from the dessert, and the tiniest speck of Chantilly cream dotted the corner of his mouth. She fixated on it to avoid his gaze.

"Look at me, Emma."

Slowly she raised her eyes and almost gasped, the intensity of his expression searing her. "The dishes," she mumbled. "I'd better..."

"Do you always talk so much when you're about to be kissed?"

Her stomach constricted. "Am I?"

He didn't answer but closed his mouth over hers, neither gentle nor forceful, but making it clear he wanted her.

She should move away, reassert the roles between them. Instead she took what he offered, tasting traces of the meal they'd shared, tasting *him*. She was all heat, all sensation. Melting like Norwegian butter in a hot pan. Sizzling.

THE SECOND THEIR LIPS MET, Nate knew he shouldn't have kissed her. She was like a drug, robbing him of all common sense.

Maybe he was dreaming. To test the theory, he did what he'd wanted to do since he first saw her. Reaching for the clasp holding her hair, he undid it as easily as he would a surgical clip.

The silken strands tangled as thoroughly as his thoughts, dimming his sense of what a bad idea this was. He didn't need the involvement, nor did she. They were about as well matched as truffles and ice cream. Yet somewhere in the world, some talented chef was probably combining the two and making it work.

Food was different. Food could be controlled. Unlike this woman, who argued every point with him, and disliked everything he was and did. Not a good recipe for a shared future. He should back away, but his body wasn't listening.

Right now the future didn't matter, he realized. What mattered was the warmth of her lithe body against him, the fast beating of her heart and the fluttering of her lashes as she looked up at him, almost in panic. Her lips were parted, her cheeks rosy. He couldn't help it. He had to kiss away that fear.

EMMA'S MIND WHIRLED. Nate's hold was pointedly light, as if to emphasize it was her choice to be in his arms. But how could there be a choice when her nerves were so fired up she couldn't think clearly?

His body felt hard, toned. A rock against her softness. She wanted to cling to him, but that would be too out of character. She was the take-charge type, efficient, organized. Never weak and clingy. Yet a distant part of her wanted this, wanted to soften.

Wanted to have someone to hold on to. Having Nate touch that part of her scared her out of her wits.

"You're thinking," he murmured, his lips moving over her hair.

She shivered. "Thinking keeps me out of trouble."

"Are you in trouble now?" He trailed kisses along the side of her neck and she tilted her head like a cat being scratched under the chin.

"I could be if we don't stop."

"If this is trouble, there's an obvious solution." He found her mouth again, his lips parting hers as he deepened the kiss. Sensation shot through her like electric currents, energizing her even as it made her want to go limp with pleasure. How could she feel both at the same time? This made no sense. It was only a kiss.

With Nate, there would never be an *only* anything, she suspected. Some men might have said her food was nice, tasty, expertly prepared. He'd compared her meal to an orgasm. Her mind flashed to what it would be like to experience a different kind of orgasm with him. She was certain he'd take his time, and her pleasure would matter as much as his own. Only when she was completely ready would he tumble them both over the edge into absolute bliss.

Oh, Lord, what was she thinking? She'd never made such a mental leap so quickly before, let alone a physical one. Especially when she knew Nate was wrong for her. "We need to stop." She forced the words out.

He was nuzzling the hollow between her neck and shoulder and driving her crazy, but he stilled instantly. When he lifted his head, his pupils were large enough for her to drown in. "I could argue about the *we*."

She looked away, afraid her eyes were flashing similar messages of desire at him. "*I* need to stop then."

"Is it the damned dishes? If it makes you happy, we can do them together."

"It's not the dishes. It's—this. I didn't mean to kiss you."

"You're not denying you wanted to."

"You know I did." Her responses had told him in every way possible short of leaping into bed with him. "The point is, we have a business relationship."

He flicked a hand through her hair. "It started there. We both know it isn't going to end there."

Emma fought to keep her voice steady. "I'm not getting involved with you, Nate."

"Is there someone else?"

She slid away from him and began to fuss with the table. "My business. My life. I don't want anything else. I don't have time for anything else."

Echoes of himself talking to Grace Lockwood, Nate thought with a pang. Was this about reaping what he'd sown? *Don't love something that can't love you back.* Did Grace's advice apply to *someone,* as well?

He collected a few dishes, feeling the urge to throw them against a wall. Frightening Emma wouldn't help. She was like an exotic creature and needed to be gentled to get past whatever fears had been bred into her. He wasn't used to his kiss spooking a woman. *And you don't like the feeling.* Was this really about Emma's needs or his ego not wanting to take "no" for an answer? He'd done it before, and lived.

His hands full, he snared her with a look. "Other people with busy work lives manage to have relationships."

*Not doctors.* The thought flashed through Emma's mind like a neon sign as she carried dishes through to the kitchen, aware of Nate close behind her. By enduring a little pain now, she was saving herself greater grief later on. But heaven help her, it was harder than she'd imagined.

Having him watch while she did something as basic as loading a dishwasher made her self-conscious, and the need to have him keep touching her throbbed through her. She had no choice. "I just can't do this. If it means you decide to hire someone else…"

"I don't want someone else," he said. "Only you."

She straightened, reaching for the dishes he'd placed on the counter. "What part of 'no' don't you understand?"

His provocative grin washed over her. "The part that's saying 'later.'"

Frustration made her raise her voice. "I am not saying 'later'—or anytime at all."

"Your voice may not be, but the rest of you is all invitation."

She tried to stand straighter, but it was difficult when so much of her felt boneless from being in his arms. The need to melt against him and continue where they'd left off was like a hunger, but she was not giving in. The conflict fueled her anger. "And the doctor is always right, isn't he?"

Nate leaned against a counter and folded his arms. "This has nothing to do with my job."

"It has everything to do with it. Can't you see? You've decided you want me, and you think it's only a matter of time before you get your way. What I want doesn't count." She arranged some cookware in the dishwasher.

"Of course it does." He sounded heated now, the teasing tone morphing into a barbed sharpness. "But short of throwing away years of medical and surgical training, and taking a job you approve of, I don't know how to get past your damned prejudices."

LEDs flashed as she chose a program, the jumping lights matching her thoughts. "You don't have to. You don't have to be anything but who you are," she insisted. "And let me do the same."

"You really believe you can have no future with a doctor, don't you?"

She swabbed an already spotless counter with a cloth, her hand trembling. The tiny movement plunged like a knife into his heart. "I know I can't."

NATE REACHED OUT AND PUSHED a strand of hair from her eyes, causing her to suck in a breath. "You know what you experienced in your family. The whole world doesn't operate the same way." It had with his father, an inner voice insisted. No, his mother had to take some of the responsibility. If she'd truly loved his father, she'd have found a way to work through their difficulties instead of walking away.

"You like order, don't you?" he asked Emma as she tidied up the ingredients she'd used for the meal. The massive refrigerator hadn't held this much food since last Christmas. The hominess of it all threatened to sidetrack him. He should get in here more, cook for himself, make his home more of a refuge. Though he'd still be missing what he suspected was the most vital element. Emma.

"Order makes it easier to get things done. In a commercial kitchen, you have to be able to put your hand on whatever you need in a hurry."

"How do you know what you'll need?" he asked.

A tiny frown formed between her eyes. "Sometimes I follow a recipe."

"And if you don't have a recipe?"

"I follow my instincts."

He picked up the bottle of rum she'd used in the dessert, and replaced it on a shelf. "Do your instincts ever lead you astray?"

"Occasionally." She pulled a face. "Not long ago, I tried making an avocado and chocolate pudding. Didn't work at all."

"Yet I had something similar in a restaurant in the U.S., and it was sensational," he argued. "In the right hands, anything can be made to work if the will is there."

Emma met his gaze, her eyes huge and liquid. "Why me?" she asked, frustration in her voice. "You can have any woman you want."

He heard the rest of the question: Why choose Emma when she was determined nothing could come of it?

He refused to think her elusiveness was the main attraction. The medical professionals she knew were probably used to people jumping when they snapped their fingers. He had a momentary glimpse of his staff treating his word as law, the females swooning when he smiled at them. Yeah, right. Grace was more likely to argue a diagnosis with him than swoon, and the rest of his team knew better than to yes-man him if they thought he was wrong. He might enjoy a little deference, but he didn't *need* it to exist.

"Don't bother answering," she said before he could respond. "Look at it like this. Not having the object of your desire for once will make you a better person."

His smile returned. "Oh, I'll get what I want. Not because I can't handle rejection, but because the object of my desire wants the same thing."

She sighed. "Do you always have to have the last word?"

"Only when I'm right."

HE WASN'T RIGHT, HE COULDN'T be, Emma thought. But she wasn't going to get anywhere arguing with him. Like her father and brother, Nate was convinced he knew what was right for her, when he hadn't a clue what she needed.

Or did he? The thought hit her hard. Before tonight, she'd been sure of her ground. Make the business fly, establish herself in the tough world of professional catering. Maybe open a proper restaurant later on. Nearly all her goals concerned her work, she noted. Nowhere in her master plan was a cure for the needs that coursed like a torrent of water through her veins.

"Damn it, Nate," she said out loud. "You don't know everything."

He'd placed two cups into a built-in espresso machine and fiddled with the controls. "I never said I did. You only have to watch a patient recover despite a terminal diagnosis to believe in mysteries beyond our understanding."

Love was certainly among them. "This late, I prefer herbal tea," she said.

Without comment he set aside one of the espresso cups. While the machine hissed and sputtered, he took a black porcelain mug out of a cupboard and began to hunt, looking smug when he unearthed a box of chamomile tea bags. "This do?"

"I take it you don't have any loose tea."

He stretched out the string on one of the bags. "Isn't this tea?"

Amused in spite of herself, she nodded. "More or less." She couldn't resist asking, "Nate, why do you have such an amazing kitchen you never use?"

"You think it's amazing? I'll be sure to tell Mitch Kelso. The design is all his."

"Mitch Kelso did your kitchen? He created the kitchens of some of the most famous restaurants in the world."

Nate tapped the boiling water outlet on the machine and made her tea. "Mitch was a patient who became a friend. You'll meet him at my party."

She waved both hands in front of her face. "Excuse me for having a fan moment. If I could have anyone design my kitchen, it would be him."

He handed her the tea and took his coffee out of the machine, drizzling a dash of milk into the brew. "What's stopping you?"

"Do you know what he charges?" She blinked. "Of course you do. He did this."

"He's not doing site work at the moment, doctor's orders," Nate said. "But he might do some sketches for a friend of a friend."

"You'd ask him for me?" She felt suspicion cloud her gaze.

"After a recent health scare, I prescribed rest, but he's going nuts without a project to occupy his mind. You'd be doing him a favor."

"Yeah, right."

"No strings," Nate promised. "That's not how I work."

Tonight had given her more than a taste of how he worked. Still, the temptation was too much. "If you're sure it's no bother, and no risk to him."

"No to both, as long as he sticks to coming up with ideas."

"I'll be lucky if I can afford his ideas," she said. "Thank you, Nate."

He sipped his coffee, glancing at her over the rim of the cup. "See, we doctors aren't always the bad guys."

"This is business. Nothing else changes."

SOMETHING HAD ALREADY CHANGED, Nate knew, as he watched her steer the tag of the tea bag around to the back of the mug so she could drink what must be a sad excuse for herbal tea. Next time he'd make sure he had the real thing. And there would be a next time. He wished he'd known sooner that his friendship with Mitch was a key to Emma's heart. Her business heart, anyway. Nate had no intention of letting the other man move in on his territory.

Because whether Emma knew it or not, tonight Nate had staked a claim.

## CHAPTER SEVEN

"The ice cream. What did we do with the ice cream?"

"In the chillers, surrounded by ice packs, ready to go into Nate's freezer as soon as we get there," Sophie said, her expression inscrutable. Emma wasn't fooled by her friend's outward calm. Under stress, she became what she called *über* Chinese.

"The praline shards are in the container next to them," she added. "You sure you don't want me to drive the van?" Sophie asked.

"You'll need your car to get to your exam tonight," Emma said. "I'm fine, really. It's only a last-minute attack of nerves. Everything's as ready as it can be." Her nerves had nothing to do with Nate himself, only with making sure the event ran like clockwork, she assured herself.

She and Sophie had prepared as much of the party menu ahead of time as they could. The last of the fresh ingredients were packed into Emma's white van for final preparation when they got to Nate's house.

"How did the tables look when you checked on them?" Sophie asked as Emma locked up.

"Fabulous. The rented dining tables are perfect, and the motley collection of old silverware and serving dishes looks like they came straight out of the family vault. The linens are fantastic—they remind me of the lacework Gramma Jessie told me her grandmother used to make. Where did you find it all?"

"Chinatown, where else?" Sophie peeled off to her car. "If we're all set, I'll see you at Nate's."

Emma got in and started the van. She drove carefully so she wouldn't shake anything around too much. Nate hadn't been at the house when she was there earlier, and she told herself she was thankful. Today of all days, she didn't need the distraction.

Things had been bad enough when he brought Mitch Kelso to meet her a few days before. She'd expected to feel tongue-tied around the master designer, but instead it was Nate who put her senses on red alert. With Mitch she was fine. They spoke the language of chefs, making her forget her hero worship in the joy of talking to someone so completely on her wavelength.

She didn't want to think about what he'd charge for the input into her kitchen design. According to Nate, she was helping Mitch by giving him a challenge that suited his present state of health, but she wasn't convinced. He looked slimmer than the publicity shots she'd seen of him, and a little hollow-cheeked. Most people would after the multiple bypass surgery he told her he'd undergone. But to have the chance to work with such a genius on any terms was worth any price he might name.

Margaret was still in Bali, but Emma hadn't been able to resist calling Carla with the news. Her friend had shrieked over the phone, making Emma promise to introduce her to Mitch or have her supply of Carla's brownies cut off. Recognizing the dire threat, Emma had laughingly agreed.

Carla worked at her current job Tuesday through Saturday nights. Since Nate's party was on a Tuesday, she'd made him a wonderful birthday cake as her contribution. Should be the hit of the evening, Emma thought. The cake had been delivered directly to Nate's house, and Emma had already taken a peek. Thin layers of flourless chocolate cake were sandwiched with chocolate mousse and hazelnuts, the top glazed and decorated with chocolate curls.

In keeping with the theme of the party, Carla had made the cake look homemade, with the layers artistically stacked off center and the glaze flowing down the sides. Emma's contribution was the cake topper. Around an operating table made out of fondant, she'd swirled patient notes written in edible ink, a stethoscope and a heart. The pièce de résistance was an edible figure of a patient in gaping hospital gown balancing on the edge of the cake as if about to topple off. His cartoon-style speech bubble, also in edible ink, read, "I can't be thirty-five. I want a second opinion."

She and Sophie wore their usual outfits of black chef's pants and white polo shirt with their business logo—a small L, a larger T and a small C for Love This Catering—on the breast, covered by a black apron printed with a tuxedo design. Practical, stylish and memorable. Emma should be on top of the world. Instead she felt as if a million butterflies had set up camp in her stomach.

The pressure of the party didn't fully explain the sensation. A lot was due to Nate himself. While she'd talked kitchen design with Mitch, Nate had stayed in the background. Expecting him to be bored, she'd been surprised when he contributed a few insightful thoughts. At all times she'd been aware of his eyes on her, practically able to *feel* his gaze. Once she'd actually touched her hand to her cheek, swearing he'd reached out to her. When she'd looked at him, he hadn't moved but seemed amused, as if knowing exactly what was going on in her head.

Such thoughts weren't helpful, she admonished herself as she guided the van through the heavy traffic. Tonight she was in professional mode, not mooning over a man who was totally wrong for her. Once she'd done her job, she wouldn't see him again unless they ran into each other at another of her parents' parties. Instead of reassurance, Emma felt a sense of letdown she blamed on having started work at dawn.

By the time she reached Nate's house, Sophie's car

was parked near the back entrance. They'd hired two waiters, a student from Sophie's study group, and one of her young cousins. She was briefing them when Emma walked in. Both wore dark trousers and white shirts, and looked the part, if a bit nervous.

Nick, Sophie's study partner, had done casual waiting jobs before. Jia wanted to work in hospitality. Both were keen enough and their rates affordable. "Do you think they'll cope with the work?" Emma asked.

"We're about to find out," Sophie said when she'd sent the two men outside with trays of cold canapés for the early arrivals. Sophie rattled off a list of items she'd unpacked from her car. "You were right about this kitchen, it's amazing." She headed toward the door. "I'll give you a hand unpacking the van."

Once everything was stored in Nate's fridges and freezer, Emma parked her hands on her hips. "Since we only have an hour before you need to leave, we'll prep the meat loaves first," she said after a moment's consideration.

Sophie opened containers, while Emma lined up the four dozen beef and veal loaves she'd par baked this morning, as well as the half-dozen vegetarian lentil-and-walnut versions. Covering them with chopped tomatoes and parmesan took little time, then they were set to bake for another twenty minutes. They'd have to stand for an additional ten before turning out and plating up. Enough time to get the salmon cakes happening, Emma calculated.

Earlier in the day, she'd prepared the mixture along with the polenta and breadcrumbs to coat the cakes. Sophie slipped into place beside Emma and began rolling the mixture into cakes, while Emma coated them and set them aside to rest. Two per serve meant over a hundred cakes. Emma felt her nerves sharpen. Even with a lot of the meal prepared ahead, how on earth was she to manage once Sophie left?

She would just do it. Pulling this off successfully meant getting her name out there with Nate's influential friends. She would be able to upgrade the kitchen all the sooner and the business would never look back. Pleasing Nate had nothing to do with her concerns.

Sophie pressed the back of her hand against her forehead. "What's next?"

"Char grill the salmon cakes and keep them warm. I'll get the rum babas underway then start getting the first course ready to serve."

The yeast cakes for the rum babas were already cooked. Emma warmed the syrup of sugar cane and rum, and poured it over the cakes, giving them time to soak up the mixture. Chantilly cream would come later, but first she needed to make the truffle dressing for the mashed potatoes. She nodded to Jia when he came in to collect another tray of canapés. At least they were going well.

The potatoes were already roughly mashed. All that was needed was to mix butter with the minced black truffles—black gold as the supplier called them—then incorporate them into the potatoes. An extra splash of truffle oil, heavy cream and seasoning completed the dish.

Several trays of potatoes later, Emma surveyed her handiwork with satisfaction. With the meat loaf and slices of the Toulouse sausage she and Sophie had spent the past two days making by hand, she'd defy anyone not to be impressed. She sniffed the rich aroma of nutmeg spicing the sausage. It wasn't always added to the meat. Only the rich could have afforded nutmeg, a fabulously expensive spice in the sixteenth century when the recipe had been created. In south-western France the sausages were simple farmhouse fare, the reason Emma had wanted to make them as part of the home-cooking concept.

From the van, she'd unloaded two banquet trolleys capable of keeping large amounts of food at serving temperature. They were already filled, and Sophie was almost done with the salmon cakes.

When Emma set to preparing the Chantilly cream, Nate's state-of-the-art mixer caused her a moment's jealousy. "I can't complain about our client's equipment," she said.

Sophie gave a snort. "You can say that again."

Emma felt her face heat. "Kitchen equipment."

"How are you ladies getting on here?"

Nate would choose that moment to make an appearance. Making an effort to meet his gaze, Emma saw amusement and something else—desire? Not when she was in working uniform and flushed from the stove's heat.

He looked great. A deep blue, almost gray designer shirt skimmed his torso, making her hands itch to do the same.

She dropped her gaze, another mistake, because it meant she was staring at a pair of snug military-cut jeans with pockets all over. The man looked more masculine than ever. The floor seemed a safer focus, but there were his feet in Wolverine style boots. She recalled hearing that when a man dated a woman, his feet pointed where his body wanted to go. His feet were pointed right at her.

Emma willed her voice to sound calm. "We're fine. How are the canapés holding up?"

Again, that look of reading her thoughts. "The empty platters should tell you how many compliments you're getting. And your mother wants you to know she and your dad are here."

Not that she'd have a chance to socialize. "What time do you want everyone seated?"

"They're happy mixing and mingling for now. Say forty minutes."

"No problem." Forty minutes was nothing. Fifty first courses, mains and trimmings and desserts. So much still to do.

"I'd be happy to lend a hand," he offered.

Had he read her anxious thoughts? "This is your birthday. Your job is to play host to your admirers." Having him in the kitchen with her was fraying her nerves even more.

"There's only one I care about," he said, too low for Sophie's ears.

Emma wasn't sure she'd heard right, either. "No admirers in here," she said tautly, "only the hired help."

"You know I don't think of you in that way."

"You should start."

He looked puzzled, then annoyed. "If you need anything, I'll be outside—with my admirers," he said pointedly.

By the time Sophie left with obvious reluctance, Emma felt as if the night would never end. As fast as she sent the waiters out with loaded trays, they returned for more. But Nate was right. The plates came back almost scraped clean.

While she was plating up the meat loaves and Toulouse sausage, a teenager wandered into the kitchen. His slouching posture and sullen expression suggested he wasn't having as much fun as the other guests. Possibly because most of them were older than he was. "Can I get you something?" she asked.

"I know my way around here." He opened a refrigerator and started to forage.

Fearing for the food she'd prepared, Emma went up to him. "The kitchen is kind of off-limits for now. If you tell me what you're looking for…"

"I'll just take this," he said, grabbing one of the rum bottles she'd used earlier to make the dessert sauce.

Before she could react, he'd shouldered his way through another door into the main part of the house. He certainly seemed to know where he was going. She jumped as Nate appeared at her shoulder. "Did Luke come in here?"

The teenager must be Luke, Nate's troublesome half brother. "He went into the house."

Without another word, Nate disappeared through the door. Emma began to plate up the main courses. Hadn't she reminded Nate herself that she was only the hired help? It wasn't up to her to get involved with his family's problems.

By the time he returned with a face like thunder, she'd sent the waiters out to the terrace with the last of the main courses, and was drawing a breath before starting to plate up the desserts. "Everything all right?" she asked him.

"Couldn't you see Luke's under age? Why the hell did you give him booze?"

"I didn't *give* it to him, he helped himself. I couldn't stop him."

Immediately, Nate relented. "He's being a royal pain tonight."

"Maybe because there aren't many young people here." When she'd checked outside to make sure everything was under control, she'd noticed Luke sitting by himself in the shadows.

"Did you confiscate the rum?" she asked.

"He'd already had a good drink. But it's out of harm's way now."

"Then you should be outside enjoying yourself. This is your night."

"It should be." He sounded unconvinced. Was the fact he was thirty-five troubling him, or was something else wrong? Half of her wanted to go to him and find out what was spoiling his mood. The other half knew she'd never make it through the night if she let herself get sidetracked. Not that she wasn't strongly tempted.

She forced herself to focus on her tasks. Nate hadn't noticed she was working alone. He was too preoccupied with his own affairs, which was probably a good thing. She needed to concentrate on getting through this dinner.

She shouldn't have worried about dessert. The rum babas served with the Chantilly cream and praline ice cream were a hit. If the guests thought they were good, wait until they saw Carla's cake.

Emma waited until she judged the moment to be right, then lit the candles on the cake, the numbers three and five. Not wanting to trust the masterpiece to the waiters, she decided to carry it out herself.

The light was already low, the tables mostly lit by candles with strings of lanterns decorating the terrace. While the guests enjoyed dessert, Emma had sneaked out and located Nate's parents, asking them to start the singing as soon as she came out with the cake. She'd met Nate's mother a few times socially, but this was the first time she'd met his stepfather. It was a shame his birth father hadn't made it to the party, but what did you expect from a doctor?

Mitch Kelso had waved to her from the next table. He and his partner were sitting alongside Emma's mother, but the seat on Cherie's left was empty. Where was Emma's father? In the same instant, the answer became obvious; he had been called away.

Her annoyance on Nate's behalf fired automatically but she damped it down. Maybe her father was the only one available. Half the hospital's senior staff must be here tonight. The thought caught her unawares. Was she finally growing tolerant of the demands made on her family? On doctors in general? Fine time for that to happen.

Emma picked up the cake and carried it out to the terrace, catching a glimpse of Nate's face reddening as she walked up to him. The singing was lusty, if a little off-key. She put the cake in front of him. "Happy birthday, Nate."

The second he caught sight of the toppling figure and the speech bubble, his expression relaxed. "Very funny. When you reach this great age, I'm going to get you back. Promise."

Not a promise he was likely to keep, since she wouldn't be part of his life in future.

"Blow the candles out, your guests are waiting." The waiters were already serving the coffee and tea.

"They can wait." He spoke in an undertone designed to reach her ears alone. "I haven't received your gift, Emma."

"I didn't bring you anything," she said in a matching undertone. She had thought about buying him something, then decided it wasn't appropriate given their relationship. Their *business* relationship. Strange how often she needed to remind herself of her role in his life.

His eyes reflected the flame of the candles. "You can't deny the birthday person, can you?"

"Easily." She handed him a ribbon-trimmed cake knife. "There's nothing I can give you that you don't already have." There was plenty he could give her, but she chased the thought away. "You'd better cut the cake, while I get back to work."

IRRITATED, NATE PLUNGED the knife into the cake as if aiming at someone's heart. "You'd think a surgeon would have a more delicate touch," someone said close by. He managed a grin, glad the subdued light hid the effort. He was surrounded by friends and family. The evening was a spectacular success, not least because of the amazing food. He should be a happy man.

One of his best friends, a well-known chef, had asked for Emma's phone number. Nate had grudgingly parted with her business card. Some friend. He should be glad Emma's business was getting some well-deserved recognition. But all he felt was good old-fashioned jealousy, and his only outlet was to stab the cake.

Once he'd made the first incision, and endured the jokes about his advancing age, the waiters took over, cutting and serving the cake. Nate wondered if Emma had baked the thing herself. If so, she was a miracle worker. She'd said she couldn't take on big events, yet had managed to satisfy his guests, and impress the food pros among them.

But what cost to herself? came the guilty thought. He realized he hadn't seen her assistant for a few hours and Sophie's car wasn't out back when he went looking for Luke. Only Emma's white van was parked next to Grace and Mike's Mercedes and his parents' car.

Hell of a time to think about the caterer's lack of help when the event was almost over. What would come next? Worrying about the grounds person who kept his garden in check? The pool guy? His housekeeper, Joanna?

Maybe he *should* think more about them. Joanna

had put up with him for nearly five years. If she hadn't been married and living out, his unpredictable schedule would have meant a lot of hours in an empty house, waiting for him to show up. Since when did he give a damn?

Not until Emma. The woman was a walking conscience. She'd managed to drill into his skull with the precision of a brain surgeon. On autopilot, he kept up a steady banter with his guests, while wishing he could go to the kitchen and make sure she hadn't worked herself into the ground.

The rest of the evening seemed to go on forever. By the time he'd spoken with some of the members of the gourmet club, conducting a postmortem on their last event, he was up to here with small talk. His colleagues and his family all wanted a piece of him. He felt relieved when the crowd began to thin until only his parents and Grace and Mike Lockwood remained.

Emma's parents had gone, her mother obviously disgruntled at not seeing more of her daughter tonight, although she must have been aware how hard Emma was working. She'd apologized to Nate because Emma's dad had left early but Nate dismissed the apology. They'd all been there, done that. He was surprised his own pager had left him alone the whole night, suspecting his colleagues might have conspired to cover for him.

Around him, the waiters were cleaning up. Nate

linked his fingers behind his head and stretched. Why had he agreed to a big party when he'd have been happier relaxing in the gazebo with a glass of good red in his hand and Emma giving him a hard time about some aspect of his life she thought needed improving?

A woman's voice jolted him out of his reverie. "You look like you got every present except the one you really wanted, Nate."

How well Grace knew him. "I did okay. Thanks for the silver scalpel cufflinks. The next patient who gives me a hard time will get cuffed to death."

She laughed. "Glad you like them. The cake was brilliant, too. I must tell Emma. Everybody was impressed. The whole night was sensational."

"Who's minding the boys? You could have brought them, you know."

"Their grandmother. Not often Mike and I get to spend an evening on our own, but they'd have been bored out of their skulls, and bored kids are a recipe for trouble."

His thoughts immediately jumped to Luke. The teenager wasn't with his parents, who had moved to a table by the pool, taking their wineglasses with them.

"Have you seen Luke?" Nate asked Grace.

"He went inside, probably playing a computer game. Want me to look for him after I congratulate Emma?"

"No, I'll do it." A worrying sensation crawled along the back of his neck. He couldn't put his finger on what was wrong, but knew better than to ignore his instincts. He followed Grace inside.

When she headed for the kitchen, he went to the den where a large-screen TV and gaming gear were set up. The equipment had been used, he noticed, but nothing put away. Typical Luke. Nate turned off the blaring TV and stepped over the consoles. Luke wasn't in the bathroom or any of the rooms he checked. Grace's warning rang in his ears. Where the devil was that teenager?

Voices rose at the back of the house where the cars were parked. Suddenly Nate heard the whump of an explosion, and the window on that side was bathed in an orange, flickering glow. One of the voices became a scream. Nate ran.

A teenager was laughing and tossing firecrackers at the cars parked near the back door of the house. A scorch mark scarred the side of Grace's vehicle. The door of Emma's van stood open and another explosion rocked the vehicle, which lit up with hectic color. Nate's first sickening thought was that Luke was the vandal, until he saw his half brother grappling with a second young man in the driveway.

Nate recognized the gang member who'd turned tail the night he'd thwarted their plans to rob the convenience store. His relief that Luke wasn't responsible was short-lived when he saw Emma trying to wrest

a firecracker from the first man. The screams Nate
had heard were her fury. She must have been loading
the van when the gang members turned up.

Nate's stepfather appeared around the corner of
the house, closely followed by Mike Lockwood. "Call
the police now," Nate yelled.

Josh pulled out a phone while Mike ran to Luke
and tried to separate the fighting pair. Nate grabbed
a metal garden stake, skimming it boomerang-style
at the legs of the man holding Emma. He turned at
the last second, the metal striking a glancing blow.
With a scream of pain and anger, he released Emma
and turned on Nate. "You friggin' bastard, this time
you're dead meat."

Nate put himself between the man and Emma.
"Go into the house," he said without taking his eyes
off his would-be assailant.

"I'm not leaving you with this thug," she protested.

"I can't deal with him and protect you."

"Who asked you to? My van's on fire."

Next she'd be trying to put the fire out. In the part
of his mind not focused on anticipating the thug's
next move, Nate had to admire her courage. She'd
taken the gang member on without a thought for her
own safety. "The van's replaceable, you're not," he
snapped.

The young punk sneered at the concern and Nate
could almost hear the wheels in his mind turning.

He thought he had a lever he could use against Nate. And damn it, he did. Nate tried to come between the thug and Emma but she stood her ground.

He glanced at her, trying to assess the danger she'd placed herself in. In the split second he was distracted, the gang member propelled one of the heavy banquet trolleys toward Nate. But the slope of the driveway sent the trolley careening toward Emma, who had backed into a corner of the house with nowhere to run. This time her scream held real fear.

## CHAPTER EIGHT

NATE DIDN'T HESITATE. He threw himself sideways to intercept the trolley before Emma could be crushed against the wall. But the heavy metal object was an aimed missile. He caught an edge, throwing his weight into making the trolley swing around. He had the satisfaction of hearing sirens, then the deflected cart slammed his right arm against the brickwork.

"Nate!" Emma's scream drowned out Nate's howl of pain. With his uninjured hand, he tried to push the trolley away, but it took Emma and Mike's combined efforts to shift the thing. Behind them, two uniformed police were moving in, with a fire truck close behind.

The wall at his back was the only thing keeping Nate on his feet. Emma reached to touch his arm and he held her at bay. "Is it broken?" she asked.

Too shocked to speak, he shook his head, biting his lip to stop from groaning. Emma already looked frightened enough. In fact she looked more frightened than she had on her own account, but he was in no shape to go there.

He saw the police round up the intruders. When

they were about to include Luke, Mike went to them and explained who he was, and the part he'd played in fending off the gang. He also gestured toward Nate, who heard his name mentioned as the owner of the house.

A uniformed woman approached him. "Do you need an ambulance, sir?"

No way was he letting himself be carted away in an ambulance. "I'll be okay. I'm pretty sure my wrist is only sprained." *Only* was a poor word to describe the pain he was in, but he kept that to himself.

"All the same, you should have a doctor look at that," the officer said.

"I am a doctor."

She actually rolled her eyes. Obviously she'd heard the stories about doctors making the worst patients. He became aware of Grace at his side. "I'm Grace Lockwood, also a doctor. I'll examine Dr. Hale," she said. *If he'll let me.* Nate he heard what she didn't say.

While the police dealt with the scene outside, he let Grace steer him back into the house, aware of Emma welded to his other side. "How can I help?" she asked.

"He'll need an ice pack or some ice wrapped in a towel," she instructed. "Ibuprofen if you can find some."

"First aid kit, bathroom off the den," he said. Pain radiated down his hand and up into his forearm. A double Scotch was indicated, but he knew no doctor would agree until they learned the damage they were dealing with.

Annoyed with himself, he sat down at Grace's instigation, and allowed her to examine his arm. "No tenderness at the base of your thumb?" she asked when she reached there.

"It's one big tenderness," he said. "I don't think I've fractured the scaphoid. Feels more like ligament damage."

Her eyes narrowed. "When did you develop X-ray vision?"

"I'll get it x-rayed. I know the drill."

Emma hurried back with ice swathed in a towel and watched anxiously as Grace finished examining Nate's arm and applied the pack to his wrist. "Nate, I'm so sorry," she said.

Breathing through the pain, he shook his head. "Wasn't your fault. If anything it's mine. The intruders are the two young punks I headed off when I brought Luke home the night we did the bay walk."

At the mention of the walk, Grace looked from her patient to Emma and back again, but wisely made no comment. "How's the ice feeling?"

"Better," he said, although the benefit was minimal. "I could use some ibuprofen, though."

Emma held out two capsules and a glass of water, hovering while he swallowed the painkillers. Then she took the glass from him. "The police want to speak to us when you're ready."

"Can they come in here?"

"I'll check."

BY THE TIME EMMA GOT OUTSIDE, the fire was out and the police had the gang members in the back of a squad car. They were taking a statement from Luke while his parents stood at his side. Mike Lockwood saw her and came over. "How's Nate?"

"In pain. Grace is taking care of him."

Some of the worry eased from Mike's expression. "My wife's probably the only one he'd cooperate with. I told the police what I saw, including how Nate came to be injured."

"Nate wants to know if they can interview him inside. He's putting on a brave front, but hurting more than he's letting on. Oh, Mike, how could this happen?"

He heard the regret in her voice. "You can't blame yourself, Emma."

"That's what Nate says, but if he hadn't tried to save me, I'd be the injured one, not him."

"And Nate would be beating himself up for letting that happen."

"You know him well, don't you?"

Mike nodded. "He introduced me to Grace when they were at medical school together."

"You're a doctor?"

"Hospital administrator. I know all about doctors as patients, and Grace will have her hands full with this one."

Emma's fear surged anew. "He thinks he's done some ligament damage."

Mike smiled. "A sprain to you and me. If the injury's moderate, he'll probably need a splint and a couple of days of cold therapy, then three weeks or so of recovery time."

She felt the ground shift beneath her. "He's a surgeon. He needs his hands."

"All the more reason to rest and give himself time to recover." Mike placed his hands on her shoulders. "Nate's one of the most brilliant surgeons in the profession. He knows what's at stake and what he'll have to do. He may not be a willing patient, but he won't put his career at risk."

"He already did," she said in a low voice. While the drama was happening, she'd felt coldly distant, but now heard her voice tremble. She suspected her knees weren't going to hold her up much longer.

Mike saw her start to crumble. "I'll talk to the cops. You go inside and sit down."

She didn't argue. The fire in her van was out, but the sight of the damage as she passed made her wince.

Inside, Grace was securing an elastic bandage around Nate's wrist. "This will hold you until you get to X-ray."

"Tomorrow," he said.

"Tonight. I'm taking you to the hospital myself as soon as we're done here."

He dropped the argument but the set of his jaw suggested he was far from giving in. Catching sight of Emma's face, Grace steered her to the couch beside Nate and pulled a throw rug around her shoulders. Her cool fingers dropped to Emma's wrist.

"I'm fine," she insisted.

Grace released her. "Luckily, I think you are. Sit still and rest, and you might stay fine."

Emma let her head drop back against the couch. "Your car doesn't look too bad, but the van is a mess."

"They can be fixed," Grace echoed Nate. "You two stay put. I'll see what's keeping the police."

Alone with Nate, Emma forced her eyes open. "Thanks for what you did tonight."

"What on earth made you confront those idiots on your own?"

His anger lanced through her. Not personal, she told herself. Men often lashed out when they were in pain. "When they turned up, I thought they might belong to one of your guests."

"Until they started throwing firecrackers. Didn't stop you, I noticed."

"All I could think of was saving my van." She suspected he knew she couldn't afford a replacement.

"Your insurance should cover most of the cost, and the damage may look worse than it is."

Like his wrist, she thought. Grace had used a scarf as a temporary sling, lifting his arm above the level of his heart. "Does your arm hurt much?"

"Starting to care about me, Emma?"

The steely-voiced question made her jerk her head toward him. "Of course I am. You were injured saving me."

"Don't read too much into this," he cautioned. "Anyone would have done the same."

But they hadn't, he had. She considered saying so, then thought better of it. He didn't want her getting ideas about him any more than she wanted to be having them. If they kept sneaking into her mind, that was for her alone to know.

Despite the throw, she began to shiver and felt his good arm come around her shoulders. Don't think, don't reason, just accept the comfort he was offering, she ordered herself. Not easy to do when his touch set her nerves ablaze.

Grace came back with one of the officers. Emma expected Nate to pull his arm away but he didn't, and again she saw Grace's speculative look. By the time they'd given their statements, Emma felt her face glowing, but any move she made now would only make his touch more obvious, so she stilled and suffered.

140   WITH A LITTLE HELP

"Right, hospital time," Grace said after the officers left.

"I don't need a hospital," Emma said, thankful
to have an excuse to stand. Her legs felt rubbery but
held her up.

"You need a ride home," Grace pointed out. "Your
van doesn't look drivable. Besides, I might need some
help with my patient."

Nate muttered something about pushy women
doctors, but allowed them to help him off the couch
and into the front seat of Grace's car. The police had
arranged a ride home for Mike to relieve his mother
of babysitting duties. Emma settled into the backseat.
She felt bruised all over and more tired than she could
remember.

Nate's parents were staying at the house until Nate
got back. They watched anxiously as Grace fastened
his seat belt, careful not to jar his injured arm. Before
she could close the door, Luke pushed between them
and up to his half brother. "You okay?"

"I will be," Nate assured him. "What about you?"

The teenager gestured dismissively. "Nibs punches
like a girl. Couldn't hurt me if he tried."

"You were quite a hero tonight," Nate said.

"If I hadn't blabbed about the party on Facebook,
Elk and Nibs wouldn't have showed up and caused
trouble."

"You didn't invite them here."

"No, but—"

"Then it isn't your fault. Got that?"

It was what Luke wanted to believe, Emma saw. His face twisted into a mask of distress. "There's something else."

Nate's shoulders tensed, but he said easily, "Spill."

"I'm not seeing those guys again."

"If they threw you out of the gang, it isn't the end of the world."

"They didn't throw me out. I told them what they can do with their gang. Doing graffiti and stuff is one thing, but they didn't have to hurt you."

Nate grasped the teenager's hand with his good one. "They didn't do much damage. I'll still be able to slaughter you at 'Dread Commando.'"

Luke managed a smile. "You and whose robo army?"

Grace tapped the steering wheel. "If you two cyber warriors have finished posturing, I'd like to see my kids again before they're grown-up." Luke slammed the car door and stepped back, his parents on either side of him as she pulled away.

"Sounds as if Luke learned a few things tonight," Emma said.

"Wouldn't count on it. He's had the chance to mend his ways before."

"You've never been hurt because of something he did before. It could make a difference."

Grace drove carefully, glancing occasionally at her patient. "Emma has a point."

Intercepting one of the looks, Nate growled, "I didn't break into pieces, Grace. It's only a sprained wrist."

"What would you tell a patient who presented with a preconceived diagnosis?"

"If they were right, I'd thank them for saving tax-payers' dollars on unnecessary tests."

"Sure you would. Then you'd order the tests any-way."

Listening to them was like being at home with her family, Emma thought, the reminder like a dash of cold water. Tonight, she'd almost—almost—let herself get past Nate's career to the man inside the white coat. When he'd placed his arm around her, she'd felt warmed more than physically.

Exhausted and upset, she was in completely the wrong state of mind to think about anything but get-ting some sleep, then sorting out the mess of her van and equipment. The attraction she felt for Nate was a far bigger mess, but she didn't dare let her mind go there in her present condition.

Every part of her ached and her limbs trembled. When Grace pulled into Bennelong Hospital, Emma felt like bursting into tears. But she dragged herself together. Nate had been hurt saving her. No matter how he felt about her, he'd have to deal with her concern for him tonight. The rest could wait until she satisfied herself he was going to be all right.

Grace parked her car in a marked spot. "One of

the perks of seniority is an allocated car space." This
late, there was plenty of visitor parking but Emma
could imagine how busy the place would be during
the day.

Not waiting for assistance, Nate levered himself
out of the car. "Take Emma home, Grace, I know my
way from here."

"Not a chance." Grace laughed as she and Emma
spoke in unison.

"The minute I let you out of my sight, you'll head
for your office and hide out there," Grace added.

"I do not hide out in my office." He sounded
pained, as much by the accusation as by his injury.
"Tell this interfering woman that you'd rather go
home," he urged Emma.

"Can't see any interfering women here, only your
doctor and me."

He made a face. "Two against one, and an injured
one, is hardly fair."

"*Now* you're injured, are you?" To Emma, Grace
said, "Let's get him onto a gurney before he turns
back into Mr. Invincible."

"Dr. Invincible to you," he growled. "And I don't
need a blasted gurney. I can walk in under my own
steam."

"Is he always this difficult?" Emma asked, as he
strode ahead of them toward the entrance.

"Trust me, this is mellow."

He looked back. "Emma's not interested."

A lot of other people were, she saw as they entered the reception area. Around her, eyebrows went up at the sight of an injured Nathan Hale turning up at one in the morning. Among the night staff, whispered comments greeted his entry, but nobody said anything to Nate himself. Which signified what? In his domain, her father was an autocrat. His colleagues respected him, but there was little warmth and he didn't encourage any. What was Nate's preferred style?

As if in answer, the atmosphere shifted and first one, then another of the night staff approached, wanting to know how they could help. "Keep this woman away from me," he suggested, jerking his head at Grace.

"I was going to ask the same favor," Grace snapped.

The sparring continued as she led the way past a suite of rooms with Nate's name and a string of letters after it on the door, steering him by his good arm when he made noises about stopping in for a few minutes. "X-ray first, then you can practice your putting in your office."

"You're enjoying this, aren't you?"

"Oh, sure, I love being back at work in the middle of the night. I hope you realize I wouldn't do this for anyone else."

He turned to Emma, his expression sobering. "How are you holding up?"

There was little point pretending, when she probably looked as bad as she felt. "I've had better days."

"You didn't have to stay."

She didn't want to admit how much she needed to be at his side. "I've come this far, I'll stick it out."

Grace intervened. "Now you're here, I'd like to get you checked over, too, Emma."

"What for? Nate caught the force of the trolley. I wasn't even grazed."

"You took on one of the thugs," Nate said. "Grace is right. While you're here, it's a sensible precaution."

Of course he would be sensible. Not because he felt anything for her, but because it was sound medical advice. She suspected she'd have her share of bruises from grappling with the gangster, but they didn't account for the one blooming in the region of her heart. No doubt Nate would have a medical explanation.

What would he diagnose if he suspected the strength of the need gripping her whenever she was close to him? Or prescribe to make the desire go away? She'd never know because he wasn't going to find out.

She wasn't falling in love with a doctor. Or with anyone in the medical profession. Her mother's injunction came back to her, *If you can't be a doctor, you might as well marry one.* What an admission of failure that would be.

NATE FELT A PANG AS HE HANDED Emma over to a colleague. She looked so fragile that he almost pulled rank on Grace, and insisted on waiting until Emma had been examined. But Grace was in no mood to humor him, and he did want to find out the full extent of the damage to his wrist.

He hid his concern for Emma in a doctorly assurance. "This won't take long. We'll drive you home as soon as we're done."

Walking away was harder still. "Who's on duty tonight?" he asked Grace.

"Amy Lester. Pity she's only x-raying your arm."

Had he missed something? "What?"

She opened the door into a waiting room. "A scan of your heart might show a hairline fracture."

In the entrance, he froze. "What the devil are you talking about?"

She ushered him through. "Emma's getting to you, isn't she?"

"She's the daughter of a friend. And a spectacular cook."

"Not to mention walking companion, and special enough to put your career on the line for her."

No use telling Grace he'd have done the same for anyone. They went back a long way, and she knew how important practicing surgery was to him. Before he undertook any physical activity, he assessed the risk to his hands. So his actions tonight had been a dead giveaway. But he was in no mood to discuss his feelings, even with a good friend. "Can we get this over with?"

Dr. Lester did a double take when she recognized her patient. She heard Grace's report of the accident, then examined Nate's entire arm and hand while he tried not to grit his teeth.

"No, I don't have any numbness in my hand," he anticipated her question. "And there's no history of previous injury to hand or wrist. Satisfied?"

She took his sour mood in her stride. "My tentative diagnosis is a grade two sprain with some tearing of the ligaments. The X-ray will tell us more."

Shortly afterward, he joined her to look at the film clipped to a board. A wet read wasn't always conclusive, but was enough to convince him her diagnosis was accurate. "See, no problems other than the sprain."

Dr. Lester frowned. "Based on your level of pain, amount of swelling and restriction of movement, I'm concerned about an occult fracture. I'll immobilize the injury with a Velcro splint tonight, then we'll do a repeat X-ray in five days. In the meantime, keep up the ice therapy every few hours for the next day or so."

She fitted and adjusted the splint. "There. Try and keep the arm elevated, and above all, rest your hand for at least two weeks."

He had a feeling she knew which treatment he'd find hardest to endure. Resting wasn't his favorite activity at the best of times. But he of all people knew that if he used the hand too soon, he risked further injury and a longer recovery time.

"I hear you," he said, lacking the fire to argue. Pain and fatigue were taking a toll. He'd done twelve-hour surgeries without feeling this wrung out. Picturing Emma so close to being crushed by the trolley didn't help, but he couldn't get the image out of his mind.

He found Grace in the waiting room. "While you were with Amy, I used the time to rearrange the surgery schedule, sharing your cases between me and the rest of the team. Did you know you're due over six months of accumulated leave?"

"Don't sound so pleased about it. I always suspected you wanted my job."

She waved away his complaint. "You can have it back as soon as you're ready. In about four weeks."

"Two."

"Three." She threw up her hands. "Why are we negotiating your recovery? You wouldn't stand for this from a patient."

"True, I wouldn't." His capitulation earned him a sharp look.

She took his good arm. "If you're admitting it, you're feeling worse than you look. Emma's been cleared of anything but some nasty bruising. She's waiting in the car."

"Then let's get the hell out of here."

As she watched Nate approach, Emma's heart did a little skip. His arm was splinted and angled in a sling against his chest, and he still looked more attractive than any man she'd ever known. From his conversation with Grace, he was continuing to give her a hard time.

She had opened the car door when his pager beeped. Adroitly, Grace relieved him of it and tucked it into her bag. "I'll take care of this. You're off duty for at least three weeks."

"I can still work, even if it's patient assessments and paperwork. And I can answer a pager, damn it."

"So can a lot of other people. You need to take more time off, and this is as good a reason as you're going to get. So start planning how to spend this windfall of time."

He maneuvered himself into the car and slammed the door. "Fat lot of good it will do me like this."

From the driver's seat, Grace threw Emma a look of frustration. "Remind this man that there's life outside of medicine."

He wouldn't believe her anyway, Emma knew from long experience with her own family. His injury wasn't her fault, so why did she feel so responsible? Because she was doing the one thing she had vowed not to do, let herself care about him.

The deserted streets echoed Emma's feelings as Grace headed down Parramatta Road toward

Lewisham. What traffic there was at this hour moved swiftly, the traffic lights favoring the main artery. Emma spoke almost without thought. "Would you like me to stay the night?" His head jerked up. She'd startled him. She'd startled herself, as well. "I mean, should you be alone in the house?"

"My parents are there," he reminded her.

"At the party, your mother said they're leaving on a cruise tomorrow. Today, I mean." Dawn was already streaking the sky with crimson.

"And they won't be canceling on my account. You're confusing a sprain with concussion. I don't need a nursemaid."

Grace spoke quietly. "Emma might be able to help. If you do have a fracture—"

He didn't let her finish. "I'll deal with it when I have to. All I need now are a couple more painkillers and a decent night's rest. Emma isn't a doctor. There's nothing she can do that Joanna can't when she arrives in the morning."

*Emma isn't a doctor. There's nothing she can do.*

In a handful of words, he'd dismissed her as thoroughly as her family had done. Except that she had never felt this wounded before. As if everything she was and did counted for nothing.

As if she counted for nothing with him.

"My street is next on the left," she told Grace, hiding the hurt under a layer of composure. She'd long ago adjusted to her family's attitude, but Nate's felt a whole lot worse for some reason. The aches from her bruises paled into insignificance.

"Will you be all right?" Grace asked as she pulled up outside Emma's terrace.

"How would I know? I'm not a doctor," she said, unable to hold back the retort.

The quaver in her voice alerted Nate. "Hell, Emma, I didn't mean anything by that."

But he'd said it anyway. "It's true, though." For a brief time, she'd forgotten where she fitted into his life, and let herself start to imagine where he might fit into hers. His dismissal had been the reality check she needed.

Before she could go inside, he joined her outside her building. How had a man with an injured arm managed to undo a seat belt and get out so swiftly? Or else she was moving more slowly than she realized. He reached for her shoulder. "I hurt you."

His touch burned through her uniform shirt though she managed not to flinch. "Don't be silly."

"Look at me, Emma."

Her gaze slid unwillingly upward. "You need to go home and rest."

"I need to get something straight first. I meant what I said—I don't need another doctor."

"You made the point very clearly." She started to turn away, wanting him to go before she revealed too much of her feelings. She jerked her arm free of his hold and unlocked the door, keying the alarm off. "We should both get some sleep."

As she closed the door, she heard him say, "This isn't finished by a long shot."

She let the closed door support her until she heard the car drive away, then walked through the darkened café to the kitchen, the one place where she felt in control. Some control. Her hand shook as she brewed chamomile tea. She couldn't believe how much a thoughtless remark was getting to her, when she'd shrugged off similar comments from her family countless times.

The difference was hearing it from Nate.

# CHAPTER NINE

"HOLY CRAP, WHAT HAPPENED to you?"

When Sophie arrived at ten-thirty, Emma was having breakfast, if a slice of toast and a cup of tea counted. A shower had helped her to wake up, but she'd averted her eyes from the mirror image of her neck and shoulder, black-and-blue from last night's misadventure. Keeping the tale short, she explained how the evening had ended.

"You sure you're okay? I haven't seen bruises that lurid since I pulled a pile of baking pans down on top of me in catering college."

Emma forced a smile. "Probably felt much the same. I passed the hospital check with flying colors. And speaking of which…"

Sophie's color rose. "I aced the oral exam. Top of the class."

"I knew you would." Emma got up and gingerly hugged her friend. "You rock."

"I do, don't I?" She pulled on her uniform apron. "We only have one booking today, the boardroom lunch. Easy peasy. I have study group at three, but before that I can scoot over to Nate's place and bring back our gear, or what's left of it."

"I'll do it." Realizing she'd spoken a shade too quickly, Emma added, "I called the insurers. They're going to assess the damage before we move anything. But I'd appreciate a ride on your way to class."

LETTING SOPHIE CALL ON NATE would have been the smart thing to do, except that Emma wasn't feeling smart. Aches and stiffness hampered her movements, and her head buzzed as she approached his door.

He opened it as soon as she rang the bell. "I thought it might be you."

No clue as to whether he welcomed her presence or not. Probably not. He'd made his feelings toward her abundantly clear last night. Better to keep this on a businesslike footing. "I made arrangements with the insurance agent to meet him here."

"Been and gone." He ushered her in. "He was in the area on another call. Inspected the damage to your van and equipment. Said there should be no problem with your claim, and left a stack of forms for you to fill in."

This close to Nate, the spacious hallway felt crowded. Her heart pounded in her ears and warmth flooded through her. "Then I don't need to take up your time. I'll take the forms and be on my way."

"Are you in a hurry?"

*To stop feeling so off balance, yes.* "I have things

to do." If she hadn't known better, she would have said he looked lonely. He was unaccustomed to having time on his hands, and a visit must be a welcome diversion. This had nothing to do with her as a person. "If there's anything you need, I could…"

NATE COULDN'T STAND this much longer. The only need he had right now was for her. When he'd finally gotten to sleep, he tossed and turned as he imagined the trolley crushing her against the wall. She was so damned delicate, she'd have sustained broken ribs, possibly punctured a lung. None of that had happened, but he'd woken in a cold sweat. If he hadn't involved her in his life, which included Luke and his problems, she wouldn't be hurt.

If there was one thing Nate detested, it was feeling helpless, and he was feeling it in spades. The contusion darkening the side of her neck and disappearing under her shirt made him ache to mend the damage marring her lovely skin.

At the same time he wanted to banish the anxiety clouding her green eyes, fix her kitchen, do whatever it took to make things right in her world.

Knowing he couldn't gnawed at him, bringing up memories he'd buried long ago. Thoughts of a baby sister turned waxen in her cradle, Nate's mother panic-stricken as she tried to locate his father, who'd been out on a call. The tempest of emotions that Nate couldn't fathom or fix after his father rushed home to find the baby beyond help.

None of that had anything to do with Emma, except the helpless part. Something he'd vowed never to let himself experience again. Reaching the highest levels of his profession in record time had helped him keep that promise to himself.

Yet here was Emma, unwittingly dredging up his worst fears. Making his thoughts go places he'd walled off, into rooms in his mind he'd never meant to revisit. Strain made his voice harsh. "Joanna went shopping for whatever the household needs."

The sudden tightening around her eyes made him curse himself. Why was it every time he opened his mouth he said the wrong thing? He could manage a team of surgeons and a huge patient workload without spreading this much discord.

"Well, if you have everything you need, I'll take those forms and call a cab."

"No."

Her gaze turned liquid, as if she were barely holding herself in check. "What?"

"No, I don't have everything I need."

"But you just said Joanna…"

"What I need now, Joanna can't provide."

Emma combed her hair with her fingers, tousling it and making him think of bed. "Nate, I'm not up to guessing games today."

He stepped closer. The carotid pulse at her neck

fluttered. Gently he lifted two fingers of his undamaged hand and positioned them between her larynx and the muscle bordering her cricoid cartilage. Instantly his fingertips detected the increased rhythm that spoke of excitement. Or anxiety. He was betting on the former.

Her eyes went round as saucers. "What are you doing?"

"Checking my effect on you."

"You don't have an effect." *None she would admit to.*

He took her hand. "Warm and trembling lightly. Definitely affected."

Her tongue darted out to moisten her lips. "This is totally unfair."

"No doubt." He didn't move, but felt his own pulse gather speed as he saw her pupils dilate. "In the Middle Ages, a physician would take your pulse at the same time as listing the names of the eligible men in your village. When a certain name made your pulse quicken, he'd make a diagnosis of lovesickness."

"We've come a long way since the Middle Ages."

"Only technically. The body itself is still the best indicator of many conditions."

"Look, whatever you think you're diagnosing, it's the fault of a scary experience last night, and too little sleep since then." Was she protesting too much? "I only came to see how you are, because I…" *Did she care about him?* "…I owe you for saving me from injury. I know I'm not a doctor, but there must be some way I can help."

"That stupid comment really got under your skin, didn't it?" He didn't wait for an answer. "It wasn't meant to push any buttons."

"You didn't push any. Well, yeah, you did. But I overreacted, too. Hell of a night we had."

"You want some coffee? I have real chamomile if you prefer."

Emma was confused. What exactly had just happened here? A second ago, she would have sworn he was getting ready to kiss her. Now he was offering tea? "I'd like some chamomile," she heard herself say and could have bitten her tongue off. She should be getting out of here as fast as she could organize a cab.

He led the way into the kitchen, which someone, presumably Joanna, had restored to perfect order. "Your stuff is packed in those containers," he said, pointing as he moved to the coffee machine.

"Can you manage with your hand?" she asked.

"This machine is mostly automatic. Shame it can't perform surgery."

He tipped beans into the grinder and got it going using his left hand. Then he brought out a package of fresh chamomile leaves. "I'll need your help with this."

"You have good taste in tea." What did it mean for him to buy one of the most expensive brands specially for her? She spooned leaves into the filter of the one-person pot he handed her. If her pulse was as betraying as he'd suggested, this would calm her down. She added boiling water. "This has to brew for a few minutes," she said, and went in search of a teacup.

He was in the way. When she sidestepped, he was still in the way. This was a large kitchen, for goodness sake. Why were they doing this silly dance? So he could corner her against a cupboard, she realized with a rush of panic. The kiss she'd thought was coming in the hallway had simply been deferred. She still wasn't ready. Would never be ready with him. That her damned pulse had reached a record high was pure coincidence.

Anxiety raced through her. He'd as much as told her she didn't belong in his world. Why would he want to kiss her then?

"You're thinking again," he murmured.

"I don't know how to stop."

"Then it's up to me to treat the condition."

If this was his standard treatment, heaven help his patients, she thought as his mouth closed over hers. Then his prescription took effect and she wasn't thinking at all, only feeling. Getting close wasn't easy with the splint and sling hampering his movements, but he compensated by easing her over to his good side, his arm slipping around her until she was cradled against his shoulder.

Heat ripped through her and her pulse hammered. She didn't care if he felt it or not. The beat was keeping time with her heart, just as his mouth was matching the rhythm of her lips, exploring and tasting in a way she'd never known before.

The kitchen tilted, the gleaming surfaces throwing back multiple images of her against his chest. Her hand had fluttered up to his shoulder, whether to fend him off or press him closer, she didn't know. She let her palm rest against him, feeling the hardness, the unsteadiness, the desire. She rocked him as much as he rocked her, came the dazed awareness. What was that all about?

One thing was certain—he'd done away with conscious thought. As she opened her mouth to let him explore more deeply, she was all feeling, all sensation, all wanting.

"Nate," she whispered against his mouth. Then she opened the eyes she hadn't been aware of closing, and saw his face. He looked out of sorts, as if kissing her hadn't worked the way he'd wanted. She pulled her head back, refusing to ask what was wrong.

NATE SAW THE HURT FLARING in her eyes as he made himself release her and step away. He'd gone further than he'd consciously intended. What about unconsciously? Was there a part of him that wanted this in spite of having no time or energy for the kind of relationship Emma was entitled to expect?

Never mind that his thoughts were consumed by the notion of dragging her out of this damned kitchen and into his bedroom, where he could finish what they'd started. The need sang like a fire in his blood. But he was in no shape for this, and even if he had been, she was the wrong woman.

That she'd felt right in his arms couldn't be allowed to blind him to reality. She probably wouldn't last as long in his world as his mother had in his father's. It would be a complete disaster. He couldn't do that to her or himself. He should be grateful the splint was keeping him from making a mistake they'd both regret.

"I'll get those insurance papers."

"Yes, you should." She sounded out of breath. And out of sorts.

He couldn't leave things like this. "Emma, I stopped for a good reason."

"I know, because I don't belong in your world."

"That isn't it. I mean it is, but it isn't why I stopped." Lord, he was articulate enough at the hospital. Why were words deserting him now? "I don't want to hurt you."

She retrieved her cup and cradled it in both hands, as if welcoming the warmth. "You think I can't enjoy a kiss without reading too much into it?"

He was making things worse, but was in too deep to stop. "When I was a kid, something happened."

"Your mother left your father. If you're trying

to tell me it made you gun-shy, I did the research, remember?"

He wasn't happy to be reminded. "Everything isn't in the research. My parents had a baby after me."

Surprise flickered in her eyes. "I thought you were an only child."

He resisted the urge to pace and started to cross his arms until the sling got in the way. "I grew up as one because my sister, Annelie, died two weeks after birth. The finding was crib death."

Emma's hand lifted as if to touch him, then dropped again. "Nate, I'm so sorry."

Unable to stand this close without touching her himself, he moved to the coffee machine and added a dash of cream to his cup, but let it sit. "My mother struggled with the hours my dad put in. He was— still is—the only doctor in a rural community of five thousand people and was on call at all hours. The night Annelie died, he was delivering someone else's baby and couldn't be reached. By the time we got a message to him, it was too late."

"What about an ambulance? The police?"

"Both were out on calls. They came as soon as they could, but there was nothing anyone could do. My mother believed if Dad had come home sooner, he'd have made a difference."

Steam from her cup drifted across Emma's face like a cloud. "What do you believe?"

"It was probably too late by the time my mother

found Annelie. We'll never know for sure. It was the beginning of the end of my parents' marriage."

"What about you?"

The softly voiced question made him lift his head. All he saw in Emma's face was concern for him. More than he wanted to see. But he needed to make her understand why they could never be good together, no matter how strong the temptation.

"I've never felt so helpless as I did the night my sister died." Even now, he could recall his sense of desperation, the wish to do something, anything to help. To bring his baby sister back to life, and take away the agony on his mother's face. He'd died a little himself that day, and only felt as if he truly mattered when he was in the operating room.

"So you became a doctor." It wasn't a question.

Settling his back against the counter, he picked up the cup and drank thoughtfully. "If such a thing happened again, I wanted to be sure there was something I could do."

"Even if you had the skills you do now, it might not have been enough."

"I know. I'm not God." He felt a smile play around his mouth. "Despite what you think of me."

"It was a general observation about the medical profession. I'd never have said what I did if I'd known about your sister."

"Don't start holding back now," he cautioned. "One of your strengths is saying what you mean."

"You're telling me I have a big mouth?"

"A very kissable big mouth."

KISSABLE EVIDENTLY WASN'T ENOUGH, Emma thought. "After what happened, I can understand you wanting to become a doctor. But not what it has to do with a kiss between us."

"I don't want to stop at a kiss."

Neither did she. "You didn't have to."

His words came at her like darts, burying themselves in her heart. "If Dad hadn't been out saving the world, he'd have been there, possibly able to save his own baby. But he wasn't. Night after night, I kept my mother company until we heard his car in the drive, and I scooted off to bed. I lost count of the meals she cooked and threw away because he wasn't on time, or was called away before he could eat them."

Except for losing his baby sister, Nate wasn't telling her anything she hadn't experienced herself. Knowing where this was leading, she had the childish urge to slap her hands over her ears to shut out the truth. "You're saying his work split them up?"

"They were already arguing over his long hours when Annelie was born. For a time, having her made things better. After she died, they didn't fight anymore. There was only silence and coldness. As an adult, I can see they had nothing left worth fighting for."

"They had you."

He adjusted the sling, wincing as he searched for a more comfortable position. "They cared for me. They still do, both of them."

Yet his father hadn't made it to the party last night. "Your stepfather does. Last night he told me how proud he is of your achievements."

"He's a decent man and he's been good for my mother and me," Nate confirmed.

But he'd never take the place of Nate's real father. At least both of Emma's parents understood the demands on the other. They didn't expect regular meals or hours, and didn't feel neglected when patients' needs came first. Emma herself was the only one who cared about such things.

Given Nate's family life, his decision not to avoid getting involved with a woman outside the medical profession was perfectly logical. Again, Emma felt the pain of being excluded from a select club. Nate was trying to let her down easy, but the truth couldn't be avoided. She didn't belong with him. She never would because of a gene everyone else in her family had except her.

What about Gramma Jessie? She didn't belong, either, and yet she'd made a place for herself in the senior Greg Jarrett's heart. Was she lucky, or was Emma missing a clue here?

Restlessly, she carried the cup to the sink and rinsed it, then turned to the boxes Joanna had stacked for her. She couldn't take them all back in a cab. "Is it all right if I pull out what I need for now, and leave the rest of this stuff here to be collected later?"

"Suit yourself."

Challenged by his surly tone, she spun around. "If it's an imposition, say so and I'll have Sophie pick up the rest this afternoon."

He rubbed a hand over his head. "It's not an imposition. They can stay here as long as you like."

She took in his gray skin and felt guilty for not noticing before. "Do you need some ice for your wrist?"

He nodded without speaking and went into the breakfast room. Following Grace's instructions from the previous night, she wrapped ice in a hand towel and carried it along with water and painkillers to the sunny room where Nate sat at the table.

The sling hung loose around his neck, and he was awkwardly undoing the Velcro splint when she joined him. "Here, let me."

"You're good at this," he said as she applied the ice pack to his wrist.

"Why didn't you say you were in pain?"

"I was going to do this as soon as you left."

*Because she wasn't a doctor and there was nothing she could do.* Well, any competent person could apply an ice pack and dispense painkillers. "It's not an admission of failure to ask for help." Her gesture telegraphed frustration. "I understand why you don't want to feel helpless, but you don't have to be a superhero, either."

He adjusted the ice pack slightly. "Must be that walking ego again."

Her lips pursed with the effort not to sigh with annoyance. "If you want to put it like that, yes."

"We're not getting involved," he insisted, "but if we did, you'd make darned sure I didn't have any delusions of godhood."

Was that Gramma Jessie's secret? Remembering how often her comments had brought her husband or Emma's father firmly back to earth, she almost smiled. But she wasn't her grandmother, one of the strongest women Emma knew. If anyone could find a way to reconcile family life and a doctor's career, Jessie could. Why couldn't Emma's and Nate's parents have done the same?

"I'll stay until the pain eases," she told Nate, "then I have to go."

"Busy afternoon?"

Glad of a way to distract him while the pills took effect, she said, "Only one catering job booked, but a mountain of paperwork to clear up."

"How are your renovation plans progressing?"

They'd been on hold while she catered his party. "The contractor is coming to quote on the kitchen tomorrow."

"Mitch tells me you were impressed with his sketches."

She nodded. "He's a genius and he knows exactly what a professional kitchen needs. But until the builder gives me an idea of cost, I don't know how many of Mitch's ideas I can afford."

"Which reminds me." Nate rested the ice pack against his wrist and fished in his pants pocket with his other hand. "This is for you."

She took the crumpled envelope he held out. It wasn't sealed so she opened it and was stunned to see the amount of the check inside. "This is way more than we agreed."

"You did way more than we agreed. My birthday cake wasn't in the original quote."

Because she'd only thought of it a few days ago. "Carla Geering made most of the cake and I did the decoration," she said in fairness. "Carla's joining the business as soon as the kitchen's ready. Since she wasn't available last night, she wanted to make a contribution."

"Carla's on your team so I repeat, you deserve the fee," he insisted. "If you hadn't tackled that young punk last night, he and his mate could have set my home on fire."

Some of the gloss went off the check. He wasn't rewarding her catering skills, but her usefulness in saving his property. "All part of the service," she said stiffly, and tucked the envelope into her back pocket.

He stood up, heedless of the ice water dripping

from the towel onto the polished wood table. "Now what did I say wrong?"

"Nothing. Absolutely nothing."

"Why is it I can't open my mouth without offending you?"

She kept her gaze level. Being offended suggested he had the power to touch her emotions, and she refused to let him. "What makes you think you've offended me?"

"Because you've gone all stiff again."

Her breath huffed out. "It would be nice if, just once, you showed some appreciation for my professional abilities."

The ice pack was shoved aside and he began to fumble with the splint. "The check is supposed to do that."

"You said you bumped it up because I saved your house." Setting her annoyance aside, she took the splint from him and fastened it around his wrist, careful not to cause any more pain. He was causing her enough for both of them.

Glaring at her as if he could read her thoughts, he shrugged his arm into the sling. "And your problem is?"

"My problem is you and the rest of your kind. All my adult life I've been put down for not joining the family business, as if nurturing people with food is a lesser calling than medicine. I think it's about time…"

His nostrils flared as he got to his feet, and his eyes held a brilliance that shocked her, while the intent in them shook her to her core. "It's about time you stopped telling me how I should treat you."

Alarm made her voice unsteady. "You don't think I deserve your respect?"

"You're doing it again, putting words into my mouth." His good arm came around her and she found herself captive between the table and his hard body. Her senses fired warning signals along her limbs, pulling the blood to the center of her body. Her fight-or-flight instincts were fully engaged, but she wasn't sure which she planned on using.

# CHAPTER TEN

Two GOOD ARMS WOULD HAVE helped, Nate thought as he felt tension ripple through Emma. But he put the only one he had to good use, pinning her in place while he set her straight on a few things.

Without asking him what he thought, she'd made up her mind that he was the same as her family, elevating medical professionals to a higher level than other people, and that made him mad as hell.

This time he didn't have to check her pulse to gauge her agitation. The set of her jaw and her gritted teeth betrayed her. But she wasn't as angry as she wanted him to think. Her enlarged pupils were a sexual response she couldn't hide. His were probably every bit as dilated, and for the same reason. She drove him wild, and not only because she thought she knew everything about him.

He felt her try to turn herself to stone in his arms… arm. Instead, she felt hot and yielding, sending answering heat coursing through him. But her tone was cold. "I suppose you think kissing me will make things better?"

Feeding him lines like that made this too easy. "Who said anything about kissing you?"

Confusion sent jets of pink color shooting across her cheeks. Good. He'd shown her she couldn't second-guess him as easily as she believed.

"I thought you were…when you…damn it, Nate, how can I have a proper talk with you like this?"

He studied her from under lowered lids. "You can't, and that's the point. This is about me talking for once. All you have to do is listen."

She made a halfhearted attempt to squirm free, the movement against his body almost his undoing. Seconds ago he'd decided to make her listen if it killed him. At this rate, the prospect was alarmingly real.

"Perhaps a well-aimed kick would make you take me seriously," she said.

He'd made sure there was no room for kicking, but in the process, put himself at a disadvantage. Having her pressed against him was proving to be more of a problem than violence. "Believe it or not, I do take you seriously. But as this is the only way to get you to hear me out, then you leave me no choice."

Disbelief radiated from her. "I'm the one being manhandled, but it's my fault?"

"How can I manhandle you with one good arm?"

NATE COULD MANHANDLE her from across a room, just by looking at her with those hooded dark eyes,

Emma thought, wishing he would say what he had to say and release her.

Perhaps she shouldn't have accused him of being like her family, when she didn't know his thoughts well enough to make assumptions. But this macho stuff was hardly likely to change her mind.

In all honesty, she wasn't sure any force was involved. She'd been off guard when he caught her against him. Now, feeling his breath warm on her cheek and his body aligned with hers, she could easily melt into his hold if she let herself. Or walk away.

"I'm listening."

A smile played around his mouth. "See? I knew I would get your attention."

"So does 'Greensleeves' when the van drives down my street selling ice cream."

"I can hum 'Greensleeves' if you want. Come to think of it, the words are appropriate. 'Alas, my love, you do me wrong, to cast me out so discourteously.'"

Her glare bored into him. "I'm not your love, and you were the one treating me discourteously last time I looked."

His expression hardened. "I don't remember calling your work a delusion of godhood."

"You know that was the vodka talking." Still, the words were hers, and she hadn't retracted them afterward.

"It's different when the shoe's on the other foot, isn't it?"

"Yes." The word came out as a whisper.

"Okay, so here's the truth. I don't believe, and never have, that practicing medicine makes me special. It's a privilege, and I count myself damned lucky to have the chance to make a difference in my patients' lives."

It was insane to feel so moved by his words. Or to want to return his embrace when she should be coming up with a snappy counterargument. "Because you couldn't help your baby sister?"

He inclined his head. "Annelie was the start. Now it's about the others who won't be able to go home to their families without medical help."

With her parents and brother, it was invariably about them. Their achievements, wise counsel, nick-of-time intervention. Unable to stop herself, she touched a hand to the side of Nate's face. Knew she'd made a mistake when she couldn't stop touching him.

Her fingers curled around the side of his neck, and she felt his strength, wanted his mouth on hers. Amazing how her self-control fled when he was this close. He was wrong for her. She wouldn't put it past him to say what he thought she wanted to hear. The bit making no sense was why he would.

There was one thing she could do that made sense. "I'm sorry for what I said about doctors in general.

You're right, it was a sweeping judgment. I can't know every doctor's motives."

"You know mine now." His mouth hovered over hers. "We're making progress."

Her lips felt dry but she refused to lick them. Afraid he'd take it as invitation? Or that she would? Alarm made her say, "Nate, I should get back to work."

"Do you have your cell phone with you and switched on?"

Strange how hard she found it to get out one word. "Yes."

"Then you're at work if you need to be."

Seconds ago, she'd have recoiled from the perceived put-down. Now she read between the lines. He didn't want her to go any more than she wanted to leave. The truth might be unwelcome, but couldn't be argued on her side, at least.

If the phone rang this minute, she knew she wouldn't be able to answer coherently to save her life. Her thoughts were in chaos, her body a mess of confused signals. The choice was no longer between fight-or-flight, but between two crazy options—kiss him or encourage him to kiss her.

With a light pressure of her fingers on his nape, she brought his head down, lifting up on to her toes to meet him halfway.

His arm around her tightened and he crushed her mouth with a hunger that told her kissing hadn't been far from his mind from the start. Her thoughts whirled. If he was playing her, she'd taken his bait willingly. Taken what he was offering, and given as much in return.

Whatever this was felt incredibly pleasurable. The fierce molding of his mouth to hers was like a dream. She parted her lips and he plunged.

He tasted of the rich, dark coffee he'd drunk. And maleness. And a sense of purpose that unraveled whatever she thought she knew about the kind of man he was.

When he wrapped both arms around her, the splint felt hard against her neck. Concern flared. "You're not supposed to use your wrist."

His eyes danced. "I'm not. I'm resting it on you."

"Is that medically approved?"

"I'll check with Dr. Lester. Much later."

Without missing a beat, he kissed her again, his good hand sliding down her body and inside the unbuttoned neck of her uniform shirt. "Lace," he murmured as he found her bra. "I'll bet it's black."

"Pink with navy polka dots." Had she really admitted that to him?

He cupped her breast, fingering the lace and triggering a chain reaction from her hardening nipple, all the way to her core. "How come?"

Dizzy with sensation, she could hardly think straight. "How come what?"

"You wear pink with navy polka dots under that prissy blue uniform thing?"

Some of the pleasure drained away. "My uniform is not prissy."

"Okay, practical and official then."

"No more than the white coat I'll bet you wear at work."

He chuckled, the low sound tingling her spine. "True. Scrubs are even more prissy, and a lot less flattering than this blue thing on you."

Belatedly she realized he was stating facts, not being critical. She'd have to work at being less sensitive. *If she was to see more of him.*

His busy fingers threatened to send her up in flames, but the weight of the splint on the back of her neck made her wonder what he could do with two working hands.

He dipped his head, trailing kisses along the side of her neck, making her arch her neck like a petted cat. His touch was driving her crazy, her breasts becoming mounds of liquid sensation, echoing the need she felt quivering through him with every stroke.

"You sure you're not busy this morning?"

"I am now." Oh, Lord, what was she saying? There was only one way this could end and she wasn't ready.

Keeping his injured arm across her shoulders, he steered her around the table and into a hallway. On her first visit, she'd lost her way and ended up in a bedroom. A very masculine bedroom. She'd paused in the doorway, fascinated by the huge bed with a camel-and-chocolate suede covering and a hint of black satin beneath. Piano-black bedsides and a vast matching headboard loomed. A man's room for a man's pleasure.

Voluminous café au lait drapes covered a floor-to-ceiling window. On another wall, a massive painting combined slashes of black, brown and cream, bringing the color scheme together. Instinctively she knew it was Nate's bedroom and that was where he was taking her.

Where he would take her if she agreed. "Nate, I don't know…"

"Your choice," he said easily, although she heard an undercurrent of tension. "But I need you to tell me now."

Because later would be too late. For her, as well. She was already in over her head, wanting him, needing him to keep her from thinking too much. *Afraid you'll change your mind?* More like come to her senses.

For once she'd gone beyond the point where sense could help her. She simply wanted. And she suspected he knew.

The bedroom was indeed the one she'd stumbled into. Her steps were far from steady, and his arm helped to keep her upright, although not for much longer.

Releasing her, he swept the suede cover back, revealing the satin sheets. "What about your sprained arm?" she ventured, her voice a complicated croak.

"I don't need my arm to make love."

"You could worsen the injury." She sounded like a mother hen, although it was the last thing she felt like. But she couldn't help worrying. When had his welfare become such a priority?

He turned to her and stroked a strand of hair away from her face. "We'll improvise."

Before she could let her mind deal with that, she heard the sound of the kitchen door opening and closing. He frowned. "Joanna's back."

Until now Emma had completely forgotten the housekeeper. Forgotten everything but how Nate made her feel. Joanna's return pierced the fog in her mind.

When he went to the door and started to close it, she followed and touched his arm. "No, don't."

"Joanna's worked for me for a long time. She's considerate of my privacy."

He might be able to deal with the housekeeper's presence but Emma wasn't ready. "I can't." She had to force the words out, but knew immediately they were the right ones. Making love with Nate would be sublime. She already had enough evidence of that. She was torn between wishing Joanna hadn't come home, and being glad her return had stopped Emma from doing something she was likely to regret later.

She believed him when he said he respected her. And that he didn't put himself on a pedestal because of his profession. None of that helped to make their different paths more compatible.

*Gramma Jessie had found a way.* The thought was as insistent as it was unwelcome. Emma didn't want to find a way with Nate. What about her plans and dreams? Gramma Jessie had written cookbooks. She hadn't tried to run a business while being married to a doctor.

Emma felt dazed, disoriented. How had she made the mental leap from sex to marriage? With Nate, things were moving too fast.

He jerked the door fully open. "There will be a next time."

Emma felt safe nodding, knowing there couldn't be a next time, although she wanted there to be. He was taking it for granted they'd continue this when his housekeeper wasn't around. How could she, knowing all the reasons arguing against a deeper involvement with him? One close call was enough.

A few more minutes and she'd have been naked in his bed. Improvising, he'd called it. Finding ways to make love to her that required only one arm. The very thought made her skin tingle.

NATE WATCHED THE EMOTIONS play across Emma's expressive face like scenes on a big screen. She'd never make a poker player. He read her desire, the willingness and then the concern at what she'd nearly allowed. He also saw her resolve strengthening. He could deal with that, too.

Not because he always got his own way, as he feared Emma still believed. But because they would fit together as snugly as his hand inside a surgical glove.

As he slipped his arm back into the sling, his body thrummed like a high-voltage electric wire. He couldn't remember the last time he'd wanted a woman as much as he did her. Whether it suited her or not, she wanted him, too.

He wanted to tell her how she affected him. Make her see that this wasn't only about sex. He also needed to assure her he wasn't interested in a lasting relationship any more than she was. But the words refused to leave his mouth.

Was he more interested than he was telling himself? Seeing her in a role she'd made clear she didn't want? He hadn't wanted it himself until…Emma.

Anger at himself took hold, freezing out the unwelcome emotions. "Probably just as well Joanna came home."

Her face twisted in confusion. "What?"

"This is a bad idea."

"Wait a minute, you just said there'd be a next time."

"Do you want a next time, Emma?"

Her exquisite eyes clouded. "Of course I don't. Do you?"

He fiddled with the sling until the knot felt more comfortable on his neck. Less like a noose. "We both know what we want from our lives, and this isn't it."

"No, I...I suppose not."

The uncertainty in her tone gutted him. "Last year there was a woman in my life. Almost married her until my work came between us. Finding out before you do something stupid saves everyone a lot of grief."

EMMA FELT THE GROUND SHIFT under her feet. He thought getting involved with her was stupid. The turnaround played havoc with her emotions. One minute he was ready to make love to her, now he was letting her know he felt let off the hook.

Hadn't she thought the same thing seconds before?

So it was all right for her to feel relieved, but hurtful when he did?

Yes, damn it. She didn't want him to be logical and sensible. He should be sweeping her off her feet and between those seductive black satin sheets.

Saving her from having to make the decision. When had she become such a wimp?

*Fake it until you make it.* She dragged her shoulders back. "You're right, of course. This would have been a mistake."

If he recognized the bravado, he played along. "If you need to, you can use my bathroom. I'll organize a cab for you."

When she nodded, he turned on his heel, leaving her alone. The turned-down bed mocked her as she opened a door into his en suite bathroom. Acres of marble greeted her and enormous mirrors reflected a woman who looked thoroughly confused. Faint whisker burns marred her pink cheeks and her eyes looked overly bright. She also looked aroused.

Emma splashed cold water on her face and hands, drying them with a fluffy black towel. For a moment she held it against her face, breathing in a hint of leathery aftershave, recognizing Nate's scent before hastily hanging the towel up.

Nate wasn't the first man to kiss her. Why did she feel so tied in knots? Nothing had happened. Once the insurance company had sorted out her van, she wouldn't have to see him again if she didn't want to.

Strange how the idea made her somehow bereft.

By the time she emerged, she'd regained her composure. Nate was on the phone. In the kitchen she found Joanna putting away groceries. The woman greeted Emma warmly when she went in to pick up her bag. "Your party menu was amazing," she said. "You know I'm not much of a cook, but I'm tempted to try making some of your dishes, if you'll part with the recipes?"

"Of course. Just tell me the ones you want. I'll give you a few tips for making them, as well."

"Thanks, I'd really like to try your meat loaf. I'd never have believed such a simple dish could taste so mouthwatering." She glanced toward the den where Nate was giving Emma's details to the cab company. "Is his lordship still in a foul temper?"

"He's touchy—not surprising, given the pain of his injury."

"He's such a bear when he can't work, and I'm a housekeeper, not a nursemaid."

"Can you get some nursing help to spread the load?" Emma asked.

Joanna shot a dark look toward the den. "If he'd let me. I'm sorry for talking out of turn, Emma. He's not your problem. I've known him long enough. I'll work something out."

Joanna was in her middle forties, still attractive, and devoted to the husband and grown-up son she'd proudly told Emma about when she first showed her the kitchen setup.

Nate came into the kitchen. "Your cab's waiting."

"Thanks. I'll be in touch about my things."

"No hurry. There's plenty of room to store them here. Your van as well until the insurance company collects it for repair."

Unaware of the strain between Emma and her employer, Joanna gave her a cheery smile. "Don't forget those recipes."

"I won't. I'll email them to you."

Nate led the way to the circular drive where a cab stood waiting. He opened the door and she got into the backseat. Nothing she wanted to say to him seemed appropriate, so she settled for, "I'll let you know what's happening with the van."

"Sure." He closed the door. She wound down the window, but he said nothing more.

As the cab pulled away, she had to wonder. Nate was whistling "Greensleeves."


THURSDAY MORNING, EMMA RETURNED home from delivering a corporate breakfast order to find the car belonging to Doug, the contractor, parked outside. Sophie had some errands to run but had said she'd stay until Doug arrived if Emma was running late. Her car was also gone.

When Emma went inside, she found him deep in conversation with Mitch Kelso. The designer smiled as she came in. "Hi, Emma, what were you thinking, hiring this crook to work on your kitchen?"

Doug's grin made it obvious the two knew each other. "Funny, he said the same about you," she countered. "Although he said your ideas might be workable."

"Barely," Doug added. "It's all very well for the

prima donnas to create works of art, but us peasants have to make them work in real life."

Mitch rolled his eyes. "How's the inspection going?" Emma asked.

The corners of Doug's mouth turned down. "I'm still checking, but you could have a serious problem here."

Her heart jumped. "What kind?"

"Asbestos." He gestured with a pointed finger. "That wall certainly has it. I'm still checking out the rest."

"Which means what?"

Mitch stepped in. "Under the law, asbestos has to be removed by a professional under strictly regulated conditions."

"I'm licensed to do the work," Doug said. "The tricky part is, once I start the removal process, legally I'm not allowed to stop until I've removed all of the contaminated material I find."

"But that could involve the whole kitchen."

He nodded. "I'm afraid so, love. There's nothing we can do except cross our fingers that I don't turn up much more for you to worry about."

"Consider them crossed." Leaving Doug to his inspection, she led Mitch into her office and suggested he sit down. "Nate will have my hide if I let you overdo things. You're not supposed to be doing any site work."

"I'm not. I was driving past and recognized Doug's

vehicle, and stopped to see what he was up to. Gave me a chance to refresh my memory of your layout. I wish you'd reconsider the walk-in pantry. I've figured out a way to make the extra room."

She'd vetoed the idea last time he raised it, and a chill invaded her again at the idea. "I don't like closed-in spaces."

"Not claustrophobic, are you?"

"Maybe. I only know I don't like being in small, dark places."

"I can make sure the storage areas have lots of light."

She chewed her lip. "You still haven't told me how much your consultation is costing me. With the asbestos problem, frankly I don't know if I can afford to have you do more than you've already done."

Mitch crossed one long leg over the other. "I haven't done all that much. A few design sketches, some floor plans—no reason to charge for any of it. I'm enjoying the mental exercise."

She should feel relieved, but instead, suspicion niggled. "Since when do you work for nothing, Mitch?"

He looked away. "It's my choice."

"Did Nate put you up to this?" Mitch's silence was a dead giveaway. "Is he paying you to help me?"

"He might have thrown a few dollars into the kitty. I wasn't supposed to tell you."

Anger flowed through her. "Don't you two think I can handle my own business?"

"Nate said you'd react this way if you knew."

"Good, I haven't disappointed you." She folded her arms. "You didn't answer my question. Nate did me a favor by introducing me to you. Why does he think he has to do more?"

Mitch looked uncomfortable. Belatedly, remembering his heart condition, she wondered if she should have waited and asked Nate instead.

"Nate heard from your mother that things were difficult for you," Mitch said.

The hairs on the back of her neck rose. "He heard that from my mother?" Each word came out separately, punctuated by disbelief. Only this morning, Nate had taken pains to convince her he believed in her, respected her. She'd been on the verge of letting him make love to her.

Her breath whistled out. Thank goodness they'd stopped when they had. Emma had trusted him. Thought he was different from her family. But he was as guilty of patronizing her as any of them.

Everything was starting to add up. His offer to introduce her to Mitch, the larger than expected check for her services and now this. Nate could hardly have made his low regard for her competence any clearer.

She pasted a smile on her face. "It's okay, Mitch,

I appreciate your help, but I'll expect an invoice emailed to me tomorrow. An accurate invoice."

He shrugged. "If you say so. What shall I tell Nate?"

Her smile became sickly sweet. "You don't have to tell him anything. I'll do that. In fact, it will be a pleasure."

## CHAPTER ELEVEN

SHE WAS UPLOADING SOME NEW recipes to her web page when Doug stuck his head around her door. "Got a minute?"

"Only if it's good news. Would you like some tea?"

"Make it black coffee and you've got a deal. Never did care for tea."

Emma went to the kitchen and made the drinks, knowing she was dragging out the task to avoid facing whatever the contractor had discovered. Asbestos was bad enough, but please God the problem was limited to this room. The kitchen already resembled a building site where Doug had moved things to check behind them.

Returning to the office, she put the cup in front of him. "I remember you take your coffee unsweetened."

He gave her a wide grin. "I'm sweet enough as it is."

Her herbal tea was steaming so she set it aside and linked her hands on the desk. "Okay, what did you find out?"

"First, it's not as bad as we feared. Only two walls are involved, the one behind the sinks and the adjacent one."

He obviously had more to say. "Second?"

"One wall of your flat is affected. I'll have to pull out a chunk of the drywall in there, as well."

Her mind whirling, she sipped the hot tea to calm herself. She had jobs lined up and she'd need all of them to pay for the work. "Does that mean I'll have to move out?"

"I'm afraid so, love. Hopefully it's only for a few days, but my team will have to seal the building off between the kitchen and your flat. Put up hazard warning signs, go in wearing protective gear, the whole bit."

She'd seen elsewhere how the process was done. Although she was thankful the café part of the building would be unaffected, how would the warning signs impact on the business? It was hardly going to inspire confidence in her food.

Worrying about what couldn't be changed was futile. The work had to be done. Once asbestos was found in a building, the law said the surfaces couldn't be touched in any way, not even painted. Removal was the only option.

Accepting the inevitable didn't mean she had to like it. "When can you begin the removal process?"

"There's paperwork to be done, legal formalities. But I can get started fairly soon. A job I had scheduled fell through."

*Lucky me,* she thought then chided herself. The builder was trying to help. No sense blaming the messenger. "I'll need a few days to work something out with my customers, but you can start on the paperwork in the meantime."

He drained his cup and stood up. "I like a woman who knows what she wants."

When he'd gone, Emma stared at the wall, her mind in turmoil. Yesterday at Nate's house, she'd thought she knew what she wanted. How wrong she would have been. Given this latest disaster, she wondered if her taste in real estate was as flawed as her taste in men. Should she have bought a different property?

Second-guessing herself wasn't going to help. Most of the buildings in Sydney's inner western suburbs were a hundred or more years old, and nearly all of them would have asbestos somewhere in their construction. The danger of the material wasn't known until decades after these houses were built.

Nor could she have known that Nate was playing with her. Assuring her his views weren't the same as her parents' was easy to believe because she'd wanted him to be different.

And just as the asbestos problem couldn't be wished away, neither could Nate's interference. She would deal with both problems the same way, by meeting them head-on.

A fine pickle, Gramma Jessie would call the situation. Emma reached for the phone, tempted to call her grandmother and pour out her heart. Then she pulled her hand back. Burdening her grandmother with her worries when there was nothing the older woman could do was unfair. Better to phone her when she had more positive news to share.

Another legacy from her parents, Emma thought ruefully. Bringing home tales of woe from school, or tears over some childish dilemma had never been the way to gain attention. If there was a solution, they'd offer it, even if all she'd wanted was to vent her unhappiness. But bring home a good grade or an award in sports and they were all ears.

Old patterns could be broken, she told herself. Maybe she would speak with her grandmother later. After confronting Nate with what she'd learned from Mitch.

By the time Emma had a chance to call him, the day was almost over. She'd exchanged instant messages with Carla, completed several outstanding estimates and updated her records on the computer. Finally she called the insurance company to arrange to collect the rental car her policy provided until the van was fixed.

The equipment and serving dishes she'd brought back in the cab from Nate's house yesterday were enough to handle the jobs lined up for the next few days. She was lucky she hadn't loaded most of the gear into the van before it was set on fire. She could still work safely on the premises until Doug started removing the wall board, since the asbestos wasn't harmful until disturbed. Apart from the vehicle, the biggest loss was the banquet trolley. For now, they'd have to manage with only one.

Like a scene from a particularly vivid movie, Emma's mind flashed back to the moment when Nate tried to stop the trolley from crushing her. Remembering the heavy steel cart coming at her, she shuddered. Bad enough that Nate's wrist was sprained, preventing him from working. Taking the full impact might have ended his career, or worse.

Knowing how much she owed him played havoc with her peace of mind. She was upset that he'd hired Mitch without telling her. But how could she be mad when he'd been hurt saving her? She just had to ensure Nate didn't meddle in her affairs in future.

She reached for the phone and punched in his number.

Joanna told her Grace Lockwood was there, and they were having a meeting. "I swear the man thinks the hospital will grind to a halt without him," the housekeeper grumbled.

Why wasn't Emma surprised?

Joanna hesitated. "Shall I interrupt them?"

"No need. What I want to tell Nate can wait. I have to pick up a rental car in a few minutes."

"Why don't you stop by afterward?" Joanna suggested. "They should be finished before long. Dr. Lockwood likes to get home on time as much as possible."

Unlike her parents and Nate, Emma couldn't help thinking. "Is he well enough for a visit?"

"He's well enough to drive me nuts telling me how to do my job. You'd be a welcome distraction."

Emma laughed. "I'll be there in about thirty minutes."

GRACE CLOSED HER NOTEBOOK computer. "That's all your case notes up to date. Your patients were impressed to hear you were injured heroically defending your lady friend."

Nate would have preferred to keep his personal life to himself. "She's a lady and a friend, not necessarily both together."

Grace made a show of being affronted, although she knew him too well for the reaction to be genuine. "Well excuse me. At the party, I got a distinctly different impression. You can't tell me you're not attracted to Emma."

"I won't tell you because it's none of your business. Or my patients'. Was it a particularly slow day, or was there another reason you felt they needed to know the details of my injury?"

She lifted her hands in mock surrender. "I'm not the one telling tales. Cherie Kenner-Jarrett's your main suspect. I think she likes the idea of you and her daughter teaming up."

"Tell me about it." He'd had the same impression when the woman worked so hard to convince him to hire Emma. Nor had Cherie tried to hide her disappointment over Emma remaining behind the scenes the night of the party. Obviously she hadn't known—or wanted to know—how hard her daughter had been working.

Grace stood up. "Before I go, I'll take a look at your wrist."

"It's fine." But he slid his arm out of the sling.

She unstrapped the Velcro splint. "Are you keeping up the ice therapy?"

"Of course." He endured her gentle but thorough examination. "And I've scheduled another X-ray in three days' time. The thought of an occult fracture being overlooked doesn't thrill me, either."

"The swelling's already reduced, and you have a greater range of movement than you did a day ago." She reached for the splint. "I don't think there is a fracture, but it's better to be safe."

They both knew that if left untreated, a fracture could lead to chronic disability. He wasn't about to let stubbornness put his future at risk.

With the splint back in place, he returned his arm to the sling. The wretched thing was already annoying him although he knew the importance of keeping his wrist elevated. Grace's examination had been careful, but the throbbing sensation radiating up and down his arm wasn't pleasant.

"In the meantime, keep up the ice therapy. Pain relief as you need it." She tipped two ibuprofen into his hand.

"Yes, Doctor."

"I'll bet that was almost as painful to get out as your wrist."

"The door's that way." He pointed. "And take your voodoo potions with you." But he tossed back the pills, washing them down with coffee.

"No using that hand until Amy Lester or I say you can. The most you should do is wiggle your fingers to keep the blood circulating and help the healing."

He restrained his impatience at being reminded of a routine he'd learned as a medical student. "Anything else?"

"Not for the moment." She gathered her notebook and papers into her briefcase, then looked out the window. "There is one other thing."

"What?"

"You know that lady and friend we were talking about?"

"*You* were talking about," he growled.

"I think she just drove into your driveway."

WHEN EMMA REACHED NATE'S house, the first thing she noticed was Grace Lockwood's car. The meeting must have been a long one. Or something was wrong. Despite Joanna's assurance that Nate was fine, concern for him pushed past Emma's anger. Had his injury worsened since yesterday?

Grace came down the front steps as Emma approached the house. "Is Nate all right?" she blurted out.

The doctor looked amused. "I checked him out under protest, and he's doing well. I came to finalize some medical matters with him, as much to stop him from coming in to the hospital as anything."

"Would he do that?"

"He'd move in and live there if he thought he'd get away with it. Nobody can run Nate's department as well as he can."

"Sounds like my parents and their practice."

"It's fairly common in our profession," Grace admitted.

"You seem to balance home and work fairly well."

"Ah, but I'm female. Multitasking is what we do best." With a friendly wave, she headed toward her car.

Deep in thought, Emma walked up the steps. If her mother's attitude had been more like Grace's, how different their family life might have been. Shaking off the futile yearning, Emma rang the bell.

Nate himself answered and she'd swear his face

brightened for a second before the shutters came down. "Come in," he said almost grudgingly.

She followed him into the house and down the hall. Emma's awareness sharpened but this time they went nowhere near his bedroom. Not that she wanted to go there. Once was enough, especially after what she'd learned from Mitch. The thought didn't stop desire thrumming through her, though, as he walked ahead of her into the kitchen.

Seeing the clutter of half-open packages on the counter, she frowned. "Has Joanna gone home?"

"Fifteen minutes ago. Dental appointment."

Why hadn't Joanna mentioned she wouldn't be here? Emma wasn't sure she'd have agreed to come if she'd known they would be alone. Too late now, and she was a big girl, she reminded herself. She could handle a one-armed man.

The man himself was having trouble, she saw as he returned to fighting with a package. "Damned frozen meals," he muttered. "How are you supposed to open them with one hand?"

"I don't eat much frozen food," she said. "I prefer using fresh ingredients. Here, let me." She had the package open in seconds but frowned as she held it up and read the ingredients. "You're a surgeon. Are you sure you want to eat this stuff?"

"I'd rather book a table at my favorite restaurant, but I'm damned if I'll let someone cut up my food for me in public, so I don't have much choice."

Even now, he couldn't see what was right in front of his nose. "You have a chef standing in your kitchen."

He looked stunned. "You'd actually make dinner for me, after cooking all day?"

"Luckily for you, I've been staring at a computer screen most of the day, so preparing a meal would make a pleasant change." It would also repay a small part of her debt to him, but she kept that to herself. "What would you like?"

"Anything I can manage with one hand."

Pasta, she decided, and began to forage. She'd provided the ingredients for his party, but still had a fair idea where everything was kept, and soon had the makings of a light, nourishing meal assembled on the counter. "You must have something better to do than watch me," she said, his intense scrutiny making her feel as if she was one of his patients.

Her irritation bounced off him. "Nope. You remind me of a dancer, the way you bend, stretch and spin around the room. Like there's an invisible triangle drawn on the floor, and you're performing within it."

The comparison would have pleased her if she wasn't here to tell him off. That could wait until after he'd eaten, she'd already decided. "It isn't such a fanciful notion. A good kitchen designer creates a work triangle between refrigerator, cooking area and washing-up zone."

Nate rested his elbow on a counter and lounged. "Much like the design of an operating room, except we don't cook the patients."

With onions already caramelizing in olive oil, she added garlic, the appetizing aroma filling the kitchen. She saw his nose twitch appreciatively. "What about radiation?"

"It isn't politically correct to call it cooking."

Having him watch her work was unsettling. And far too intimate. She began to chop some cooked chicken she'd found in the fridge. The meat went into the oil with canned tomatoes, tomato paste, chopped mushrooms and pitted olives.

Fresh basil and oregano would have been better, but she settled for the dried versions he had available. After tasting and seasoning the sauce, she increased the heat to thicken and reduce the liquid. In another saucepan, she added pasta spirals to simmering water.

"I'm making enough so you can have leftovers tomorrow," she told him.

"The way this meal smells, there won't be any. What are you making?"

"It's a traditional Italian dish called *pasta puttanesca*."

He grinned. "Does that mean what I think it does?"

"Harlot's pasta," she translated. "Supposedly made by the ladies of the night after work. They could throw together whatever ingredients they had on hand, and the meal didn't take long to make."

"Hmm."

"What does 'hmm' mean?"

"You don't want to know."

"If you're comparing me to a lady of the night..."

"Only in the sense of how much I'd like to take you to bed with me."

This was dangerous ground. "Before or after the pasta?"

"Decisions, decisions."

She aimed a dish towel at him but he ducked and the cloth sailed over his head. The pasta began to bubble and she moved quickly to turn down the heat. She was sure he had only mentioned bed to get under her skin, or perhaps pay her back for running away yesterday.

"You could do something useful like set the table," she suggested.

"You're staying, of course."

She hadn't planned to, but suspected he wouldn't eat unless she agreed. And good food was healing. "There's plenty here. I may as well."

He opened a drawer and took out knives and forks. "Try not to sound so enthusiastic."

"I didn't know I'd be cooking dinner *and* eating it."

"With me. That's what you're not saying, isn't it?"

She tested the pasta for tenderness. "Yesterday we agreed not to get involved."

At the door to the breakfast room, he swung around. "Sex doesn't have to come with involvement."

"To me it does."

Muttering something she didn't catch, he went into the other room and she heard him slamming things down on the table. Her heart was thumping at just the idea of going to bed with him. Not that she would, of course. She'd already made up her mind before discovering what else Nate had been up to. So why did the right decision feel so wrong?

She drained the pasta and added it to the sauce, stirring until the spirals were nicely coated. In his fridge, she'd found a wedge of fresh parmesan cheese and shaved some into a bowl ready for serving. By the time he came back into the kitchen, she had filled two deep bowls with pasta.

"Table's ready," he said.

She almost echoed his earlier words, *try not to sound so enthusiastic,* but didn't want to get back on a personal level. Better to keep things as business-like as possible between them. "If you can bring that basket of rolls, I'll carry the bowls through."

Opening the door with her hip, she kept it braced until he'd walked past her, then let it swing shut as she placed the pasta and shaved cheese on the table. To her surprise, a red candle flickered in the center. How had he lit it one-handed? Then she saw the lighting wand on a side table. "What's the occasion?"

"I wouldn't have bothered for *cuisine de cardboard*. Good food seems to need the atmosphere."

Touched in spite of herself, she took the seat he held out for her. "I'm glad you think my food is good."

He sat down across from her, raising a glass of water in a toast. "Better than good, it's superlative."

The way he attacked the pasta should have reassured her, but there was still the question of why he'd interfered in her business. She ate her own meal in thoughtful silence, the breaking of bread the only sound between them for some time.

He mopped up the remnants of sauce with a piece of bread, then looked at her across the table. "Okay, spill."

She finished the last mouthful and put her bowl aside. "What?"

"You know what. I said or did something to make you mad at me again. That's becoming a habit."

"I'm not mad at you. Well, I am."

"Then spill."

Cooking for him, eating with him were mistakes. Letting him eat his frozen whatever-it-was would have set a more appropriate tone for what she wanted to say. "Actually I came here on business."

With his good hand, he stacked the dishes into a pile.

"I told you there's no rush to collect your stuff, unless there's something you need urgently," he said.

"Sophie will come for the equipment tomorrow." Emma hadn't allowed for the distracting effect Nate was having on her. Telling herself that her response to him was purely physical didn't make it any easier to confront him. "On the way here, I picked up a rental car, but it's too small to hold much of my gear."

When he'd let her in, he must have seen the compact hatchback parked in the driveway. "Couldn't they have given you something larger? You'll find it a challenge supplying your clients in that little thing."

"It doesn't look as if that will be my problem."

"Why not?"

She hadn't intended to share her worries with Nate. Thanks to her mother speaking out of turn, he'd already tried to do too much on her account. "Today my builder found asbestos in the kitchen walls and in one wall of my flat."

Nate leaned back in his chair. His strained expression reminded her that he was far from well.

"Tough call. When builders at the hospital found asbestos in an old storage facility, they had to close an entire wing down. Seeing the experts go in all suited up in white and wearing respirators was like something out of a science fiction movie."

"Except this is real." And her home and income were at stake.

Putting two and two together, he asked, "How will you keep your business going while the cleanup takes place?"

She had no intention of telling him how adrift she felt. Not when he was more involved in her affairs than he had any right or need to be. "I'll manage."

"If there's any way I can help—"

"Thank you, but no," she cut in. "As I found out today, you've already been far too helpful."

His eyes darkened. One thing she granted Nate, he was quick on the uptake. "Mitch Kelso."

"Don't blame Mitch. I dragged the truth out of him." She leaned forward. "What were you thinking, paying him to work for me without telling me?"

At least Nate looked embarrassed. "I probably should have told you, but you made such a big deal out of how expensive he is."

Her anger swelled afresh. "I suppose making me into a charity case helped you feel superior."

"There's no charity about it, Emma. And I thought we sorted out the superiority thing yesterday."

"I did, too, until I found out what you'd been up to behind my back."

Nate got to his feet. "Paying Mitch to work on a project he's enjoying is more like therapy for him than going behind your back."

"If you'd told me that from the start, I might have

believed you. But you never meant me to find out, which is sneaky and contemptible. When I started to add up the small things, like the increased amount on your check—I'll be returning the excess, by the way—and Mitch's involvement, the pattern became clear. You think you can run my business better than I can."

He dragged his left hand over his hair. "How the devil do you reach a conclusion like that? All I did was try to help."

"The way my parents have tried to help all my adult life. With no consideration for what matters to me, and no respect for my achievements."

He looked frustrated. "I can't see what's pushing your buttons, Emma. Yesterday I thought we'd reached a new understanding."

"I did, too." Her sharp tone conveyed how disheartened she was to find they were farther apart than before.

As Nate prowled around the room, conflict raged through her. Despite all logic, she ached to be held against him, his seductive mouth on hers. Wanted much more if she was honest.

How could she feel so attracted to Nate when he thought he knew better than she did what was best for her? "What happened yesterday was a mistake," she said, wondering which of them she hoped to convince. "It won't happen again."

Pausing, he grasped the back of a chair. "You

know that's bull. It happens whenever you and I are in the same room. Tell me you don't feel the sexual tension between us right now?"

"Of course I don't." But her blood was racing through her veins like wildfire.

His next words stunned her. "You mean you don't want to. Damn it, what makes you think I do?"

Resentment rocked her. Not only did he share her parents' disdain for her life choices, he didn't want to be attracted to her, either. Shouldn't she be relieved? Instead she felt a sense of rejection deeper than anything her family had inflicted. That was becoming a habit with him. "I'm glad we understand each other," she said, striving to keep her voice level.

His expression darkened. "Unlikely. Hasn't it occurred to you that you're not the only one committed to what you do?"

This time she did push herself to her feet. "Believe me, I've had a doctor's commitment drummed into me for most of my life."

"I'm not talking about being a doctor. I'm talking about saving lives, being able to help."

Her shoulders lifted. "Is there a difference?"

"The difference is between doing something for status and recognition, and doing it because it needs to be done."

She thought of Joanna's comment on the phone. "And of course, only you can do it."

"Far from it. Grace made it clear that my department will power along very well until I'm fully recovered."

Emma looked for signs of resentment, surprised to find none. Her puzzlement must have shown because Nate added, "We still have to deal with what's between us. Basically, I can see two choices."

Warily, she met his gaze. "What's number one?"

"We go to bed right now."

## CHAPTER TWELVE

EMMA WAS SPEECHLESS. They seemed to be on a merry-go-round—covering the same ground yet unable to get off. "How is sleeping with you supposed to help?" she asked, genuinely confused.

"A famous writer once said the best way to deal with temptation is to give in to it."

"I can't wait to hear what's behind door number two."

"We go cold turkey. Kill what we feel with neglect."

Swallowing was suddenly a challenge. "That might be the safest way."

He swiveled to face her. "You like the safe way, don't you, Emma?"

"If I did, I would never have gone into business for myself." *Or be having this discussion.*

"I'm talking about emotionally. Dealing with ingredients is easier than dealing with people," he said.

"I deal with people all the time. Not only staff and suppliers but clients." Was he still suggesting she had it easy? "Why don't you say what you mean."

"Okay. Looks to me like you've invested so much energy into *not* being like your parents that you haven't taken the time to decide who Emma Jarrett really is."

Clearing the table gave her hands something to do, although she had to fight the temptation to aim a dish at him. She was reeling with resentment. "All this because I don't want to make love with you?"

"How would you know whether you do or not? Finding out would mean breaking down the wall you've built around your feelings."

"Now I'm frigid, as well. Charming." She pushed past him to carry the dishes into the kitchen, where she dumped them on the nearest counter.

"How the hell did you arrive at frigid from what I said?" he demanded, hard on her heels. When she didn't respond, he took her arm and turned her around. "Do I have to kiss you again to get that crazy idea out of your head."

This close, he made her skin heat and her head spin. Hardly frigid. "What's the point if I don't have any feelings?"

"Walling them off doesn't mean you don't have them. Yesterday when I kissed you, I saw the cracks appearing—until Joanna came back and you got cold feet."

"I did not get cold feet. To me, sex isn't a spectator sport."

"I told you Joanna respects my privacy."

Emma avoided stating the obvious, that the house-keeper would be well aware of what was going on behind Nate's closed bedroom door. "How come we've shifted the discussion to my shortcomings, instead of your interference in my work?"

To her surprise, he calmed down. "You're right, I shouldn't have hired Mitch without telling you."

From experience with her family, she knew this was as close to an apology as she was likely to get. She decided to be gracious. "Thank you. For the admission, and for trying to help. I've asked Mitch to send me an invoice. Besides, nothing more can be done before the asbestos is dealt with."

Nate was silent, but Emma knew what he would say next. "Why don't you run the business from here until the asbestos is gone?"

Sophie would be ecstatic. But what about her? She was sick with worry about how to keep the business going during the removal, but did she want to be close to Nate on a daily basis? "What would you get out of it?" she asked warily.

"Home-cooked meals until I can use my hand."

"Is that it?"

"You'd be doing me a huge favor. You saw what was supposed to be my dinner tonight. Joanna's the first to admit she's no cook." He spread his good hand, fingers wide apart. "You'll need a place to stay, as well. You could use the housekeeper's suite."

Joanna lived out, Emma knew. But she was still

hesitant. "Taking into account what you've paid Mitch, I'd still be getting the best of the deal."

"I'm prepared to call it even, if you are."

Since she couldn't see too many other ways of keeping up with her commissions and paying her bills, she nodded. "All right then. It's a deal."

She noticed his pallor and the lines of pain bracketing his mouth, appalled that she'd forgotten his injury. "There is one condition."

He reached into a cupboard and pulled out a bottle of pain pills. She took it from him and opened the bottle, shaking out two capsules. "What's the condition?" he asked.

She filled a glass with water and gave it to him. "By day I run my own show."

His eyes gleamed. "And by night?"

"We lead our separate lives."

He swallowed the pills. "You think I can't keep my hands off you if you're living under my roof?"

How could he be sure, when she wasn't? "It isn't a challenge. But we need some ground rules. I need some rules." She couldn't function professionally and deal with the way she practically went up in flames with little more than a touch. "I won't deny there's… chemistry…between us. But we don't have to give in to it."

"Unless we both agree," he added.

She felt safe inclining her head. "No more thinking you know what's best for me."

He gave her a rueful grin. "I try not to make the same mistake twice. Next time I'll ask."

That was a start. "Then this could work. When Doug's ready to start removing the asbestos, I'll let you know. Should be in the next few days. In the meantime, I'll cook dinner each night for you as part of our deal."

"I'll look forward to it."

So would she, but she avoided examining her reasons too closely. She'd stated her rules, and would abide by them. *If it killed her.*

NATE SAW HER OUT, THEN SANK onto the sofa in the den, waiting for the pills to kick in. He told himself having Emma in his house wasn't the reason for his spirits lifting, although he'd needed some good news. In a couple of days he'd have the second X-ray to find out whether the first scan had missed an occult fracture. If it had, he'd be out of action for months instead of weeks. And he was already going stir-crazy.

Keeping the peace between them would be a challenge. He couldn't even do Emma a favor without setting her off like a firecracker. Paying Mitch when she obviously couldn't afford the designer's services had seemed like a nice thing to do. Where did she get off attributing his gesture to some kind of arrogance peculiar to doctors?

He hated feeling like a lowlife for going behind her back. But he'd seen how defensive she was about her work and, knowing her parents, he shouldn't be surprised. Cherie and Greg Jarrett had inflated ideas about medicine. As visiting medical officers at Nate's hospital, they were notorious for resisting policies designed to make the senior medical staff more approachable.

Nope, Nate couldn't blame Emma for having a chip on her shoulder. He could and did blame her for lumping him in with her family. Okay, she had a point about Mitch. But surely Nate wasn't totally self-important? He was fallible, human.

Miserable.

The pain in his wrist was only part of his discomfort. The rest had to do with Emma. She was making him miserable. No, scratch that. *He* was making himself miserable because she haunted his thoughts, gave him an outback-size erection at the most inconvenient times and made him wish he was different.

He didn't want to be different. He'd worked hard to get where he was and shouldn't have to apologize for his achievements. If she didn't like it, too bad. When she moved in, she'd better get used to taking him as he was. He'd defended himself to her for the last time.

COOKING AN EVENING MEAL for Nate was very different from moving into his house, Emma thought as she unloaded cases from the rental car. For the past two days she'd managed to be pleasant but aloof when she'd come to prepare his dinners, and he'd responded in kind.

Under protest, she'd agreed to eat with him. For company, he'd said. He had no idea how unsettled she felt sharing his table. Simple requests for salt or cream for coffee brought images of him doing the same with a wife someday. Emma wasn't interested in the role, but the idea of another woman sitting opposite him was unaccountably upsetting. It hurt almost as much as finding out he'd been paying Mitch without telling her.

Nate wasn't going to change no matter what he said. She'd be a fool to let herself regard him as anything but a client. Not that she let her clients kiss her. When she thought about his seductive mouth on hers, just the memory made her reel.

Apart from the weather, their only conversation was when she asked about his wrist, or he complimented her on the food. He was following her rules to the letter. Why, then, did she feel so on edge?

Some people just didn't know what they wanted, she chided herself. She didn't need him interfering in her affairs, and she certainly didn't want closeness between them. If the result was a feeling of general dissatisfaction, she'd have to live with it.

So would her mother. Emma smiled. After toying with not telling her family where she'd be living, she concluded they'd find out via the medical grapevine if nothing else. Naturally, Cherie had Emma engaged to Nate before she'd finished explaining what was going on.

Mitch had looked amused when she told him she'd made a deal with Nate. "I'm betting he won the argument."

"There was no argument. I agreed to let Nate pay for the work you've done so far, and in return I'm cooking for him until he can fend for himself."

"There's a first time for everything," Mitch muttered. At her baffled look, he went on, "I've never heard anyone say Nate couldn't fend for himself. He's one of the most self-sufficient people I know."

"Haven't you heard the saying about no man being an island?"

"You haven't seen the good Dr. Hale in his element, at the hospital. His word is practically law."

One reason why she was determined to keep her cool. She'd had more than enough of her parents throwing their professional weight around. She had no wish to see Nate do the same. She hated to think she was still deluding herself that he was somehow different. When would she learn?

Probably over the next few days, she concluded, depositing the last of her things in the housekeeper's suite. Nate might be able to keep up his good guy act for a short time, but living and working under his roof, Emma was bound to see his true colors. By the time she could return home, she should be well and truly over any delusions about Nate. Strange, but the idea gave her no satisfaction.

Her rooms were located at the opposite end of the house from his. The suite comprised a spacious bedroom with an en suite bathroom, a sitting room with a plasma TV on one wall and French doors leading to a private terrace. Opening the doors, she breathed in the scent of old-fashioned roses. Too bad she wouldn't have much time to enjoy the outdoor area. According to Doug, her home would be cleared as safe within a few days, provided he didn't find any more problems.

Joanna had said Nate was having the second X-ray on his wrist today. Emma told herself she was glad of the chance to settle in without having Nate around. But after putting her clothes and personal items away, and setting up her computer in the sitting room, she found herself clock watching. How long did one X-ray take, anyway?

NATE LEANED BACK IN HIS CHAIR to sniff and sample the jewel-colored cabernet shiraz the waiter poured for him. When he nodded his approval, the man left. "There's one thing to be said for not being able to drive."

His friend Troy Lawler frowned at his glass of sparkling water. "All right for some." He picked up the glass. "To your X-ray showing no sign of a fracture."

Nate raised his own glass. "I'll drink to that." He didn't want to admit how worried he'd been that the second X-ray would reveal more damage than the first. He hadn't relaxed until Amy Lester had given him the all-clear. "Your timing was perfect, Troy. When you called to suggest lunch, I was getting into a cab outside the hospital."

His friend grinned. "Naturally. Timing's my specialty."

"So's modesty." But Troy was right. As a Formula One driver, he'd been crowned world champion three times in a stellar career driving for Team Branxton. Three years ago, Troy had been staying at a winery outside Canberra when Nate's gourmet group had arrived for lunch. After asking the winemaker to introduce them, Troy had become an occasional member of the group. His friendship with Nate had developed in tandem, and they made a point of getting together as often as their work allowed.

Troy watched the waiter serve the *mezze* they'd ordered, a combination of hummus, baba ghanoush, *labneh,* pureed peppers, walnuts and breadcrumbs, a generous serving of warmed pita bread and fresh mint leaves as a palate cleanser. "I hear your birthday dinner was spectacular. Shame I was in Spain and had to miss her."

About to sample the creamy *labneh* served with salt, red pepper and olive oil, Nate paused. "Excuse me?"

Troy bit into a chunk of serrano pepper. "News travels fast. Your lady chef is...wow, hot."

"I assume you mean the pepper?" Nate said, keeping his tone neutral.

Troy cooled his mouth by tasting the *labneh*. "Word is she's hot, too."

Since many of their friends had attended the dinner, Nate was left wondering who'd been talking. "Emma wasn't hired for her looks. She's a top-notch caterer."

"And hot. I looked her up on the Net."

"Because?"

"I wanted to see who'd caught your eye. You have to agree, it's been a long time between drinks."

Nate balled his good hand into a fist, keeping it out of sight under the table. "Good to know you're keeping score."

"Out of concern for your well-being, my friend."

"I'm touched. Now can we drop the subject?"

Troy reached for more pita bread. "Hey, this woman's really important to you, isn't she? When do I get to meet her?"

There was no way around it. "She'll be at the house when you drop me home."

The other man's eyes widened. "She's living with you?"

"Not in the way you think." Nate explained about the asbestos problem.

Troy looked unconvinced. "There are lots of ways to help without setting up house together."

"We haven't set up house, damn it. For the time being, Emma's my live-in cook."

His friend only smiled.

Nate was glad when Troy switched his attention to the meal. Emma wasn't important to Nate and she didn't want to be. Fine by him. He didn't need the complication, either. Nor was he thrilled to have his friends discussing his love life behind his back. Not that Emma was part of his love life.

In an attempt to stop his thoughts going round in circles, he drained his wineglass, intercepting a look from Troy. "Now what?"

"Nothing. I was thinking this *mohammara* is excellent. Does your Emma cook Lebanese food?"

"She can cook anything she sets her mind to," Nate said, then realized he'd missed the key part of the question. "And she isn't my Emma."

A waiter brought more pita bread and a dish of slow-cooked fava beans known as *fool,* richer and meatier than the fruit-based European dish of the same name. But Nate's appetite had vanished. He wished there were some way to get out of Troy driving him home. He could imagine the other man's response if he tried. Nate might as well announce his engagement to Emma.

Now there was an image he didn't need. After his disastrous near-engagement to Pamela, he should have learned his lesson. Pam had been turned off by his lifestyle quickly enough. Emma was already antidoctor, so there was even less chance of anything happening between them.

Putting his ring on her finger made no sense. Yet the notion persisted. The only explanation must be his injured state. If his wrist wasn't so tender after the X-ray and Amy's examination this morning, he wouldn't be so vulnerable. Since he'd cut back on the painkillers, what he needed was another glass of the excellent red.

"Easy on that stuff," Troy cautioned, watching him refill his glass.

"Why? I'm not driving."

"Emma might not be happy if I have to carry you home."

"You won't." Nate took a defiant swallow, then asked himself what he was defying.

Troy toyed with his water glass. "If she does have a hold on you, is it really so bad? And don't tell me she doesn't. I've never seen you this uptight over any woman."

Slowly Nate lowered the glass. "Okay, Emma's attractive and sexy as hell. But she's not looking for a relationship any more than I am."

"You're thirty-five. You don't want a wife and family?"

"I didn't say that. I said she's not the one."

"So the attraction's all on your side?"

"Yes." As soon as he spoke, Nate saw the trap. "She hates doctors."

Troy grinned. "How about racing drivers?"

"I won't always have this sling," Nate grumbled.

"Spoken like a man who's got it bad." Troy leaned closer. "You know what your trouble is?"

Nate kept a tight rein on his temper. "I'm sure you're going to tell me."

Troy nodded. "You became a doctor so you could fix the world. This woman has a problem you're afraid you can't fix, so you're going to back off."

"How the hell do I fix a lifelong dislike of the medical profession?"

"By showing her you aren't all alike. And making her want you as much as you want her."

"Is it that obvious?"

"Painfully. Look, when I started to race, a more experienced driver told me you can't set records with your foot on the brake. It's time you took your foot off the brake, too. Either that, or pull into the pit and let the better man lap you."

In spite of himself, Nate's mouth twitched. "Go to hell, Troy."

His friend laughed. "Right behind you, buddy."

EMMA TOLD HERSELF SHE WASN'T listening for Nate's return. Mixing the sticky dough to make rum and raisin brownies was a good way to work off her frustration at being exiled from her business, not to distract her because she was worried about him.

She packed the mixture into a catering-size baking pan and placed it in the oven then looked around the kitchen. She'd cooked a roast vegetable frittata for dinner. The spicy chicken salad, savory tartlets, *arancini* balls and fancy cupcakes for tomorrow's job were done. Where the devil was Nate?

The brownies were cooling and she was cleaning the kitchen by the time she heard a car pull into the driveway. Glancing outside, she gave a low whistle at the sight of the gleaming red Ferrari. A dark-haired man climbed from the driver's seat, giving an impression of strength and purpose. He looked familiar, she thought, watching him walk around to the passenger side and help Nate out of the low-slung vehicle.

Joanna reached the front door before her. "Do you need any help, Nate?" she asked.

"I'm fine, thanks. Did Emma get settled in?"

Emma stepped out from behind the housekeeper. "Hours ago." Hearing the disapproval in her voice, she added, "Joanna told me you were having the second X-ray, so I went ahead and moved into the housekeeper's suite. I hope that's all right."

"It's what we agreed, isn't it?" Was it her imagination or did he walk up the steps less steadily than usual? Her heart flip-flopped. She moved aside to let him come in, aware of being appraised by the dark-haired man who'd brought Nate home.

He offered her his hand. "I'm Troy Lawler. You must be Emma. Good to meet you."

His grip was like iron. Then it came to her where she'd seen him before. On the winner's podium. He was a famous racing driver. "Pleased to meet you, too."

"Is Nate…" She was almost afraid to ask.

"He's fine. We had a rather long lunch."

Nate had been drinking? She would have been angry with herself for caring about him if she hadn't been so relieved that he was otherwise all right. "Then the X-ray came out clear?"

"As a whistle."

"Thank God," she said, almost to herself.

"Some coffee might be a good idea," Troy suggested.

Glad of something useful to do, she headed for the kitchen, hearing Nate and Troy talking as they went into the den.

Joanna joined her in the kitchen. "Did Troy just say Nate's wrist isn't fractured?"

Emma busied herself with the coffee machine. "The X-ray came out clear."

"Just as well. If he stays away from the hospital for much longer, I might have to hurt him myself."

But the shaky smile she shot Emma told its own story. The housekeeper had been worried about Nate, too. Too? Okay, so it was natural to be concerned about a friend. That didn't mean anything else was going on. "How does Troy like his coffee?" she asked.

"Black, strong, three sugars," Joanna supplied.

"Three?"

"He says he needs the energy."

To Emma, the racing driver looked like a bundle of barely leashed energy as it was. Maybe it was the caffeine.

"Now we know it's good news, I can head home for the day," Joanna said.

When the housekeeper had gone, Emma made the coffee along with Nate's macchiato, and carried them to the den.

Nate sat on the couch, his feet planted wide apart. Troy was perched on the arm of a chair. Both thanked her when she delivered the coffee, but as she turned to go, Nate said, "You're not the hired help, Emma. Why don't you join us?"

"Yes, join us, Emma," Troy echoed.

"I'll get myself some tea."

She was back in minutes with a cup of herbal tea. The only place she could put her cup within reach on the coffee table was beside Nate. Awareness of him shot through her as she settled into a corner of the sofa. "I've followed your career for years," she told Troy.

"And?"

Not sure what he expected, she added, "I don't know how you manage to go so fast."

"Sometimes too fast," she heard Nate mutter.

Troy pointedly ignored the gibe. "Have you ever been trackside during a race?" She shook her head. "If you ever want to, I'll arrange a VIP pass for you when I'm racing."

"Thanks, it might be fun, after seeing you on television."

He gave a theatrical sigh. "Story of my life. All the beautiful women are watching me at home."

She seriously doubted he was short of female company, not looking the way he did and with a profession most women regarded as a turn-on. There was no doubt he was an attractive man, but he wasn't… Nate.

"What did Dr. Lester say about your arm?" she asked to divert her thoughts.

"She says I'll live. No sign of an occult fracture."

"That's good news, isn't it?" He didn't sound as pleased as she would have expected.

He nursed his coffee. "Depends."

"Aren't you keen to get back to work?"

"Of course. But I won't have full use of my hand for two or three more weeks."

What was going on here? Was it the wine talking? She couldn't believe he actually wanted more time to himself. Up to now, she'd thought he was chafing at the bit to return to performing surgery, but it sounded more like he enjoyed having an excuse to stay home.

If she hadn't known better, she'd think he wanted to be with her. She stood. "I'd better get back to the kitchen. Will you be staying for dinner, Troy?"

"Yes," he said.

At the same moment, Nate said, "No."

The racing driver shrugged. "Looks like I'm outvoted."

Nate nodded. "Thanks for the ride home. Don't slam the door on your way out."

## CHAPTER THIRTEEN

AFTER THE OTHER MAN LEFT, Emma's look went to Nate. "Wasn't that a bit harsh?"

"I've had a god-awful day. I'm in pain. And yes, it probably was. Troy can cope, so don't waste your concern on him."

"I'm not. I'm more worried about what's got into you. You've been in pain for days and it hasn't turned you into such a bear. How much did you have to drink at lunch?"

"Three glasses of red wine. Clinical symptoms—mild euphoria, decreased inhibitions, diminution of judgment and control, mild sensory-motor impairment."

"And rudeness to your friends, evidently. Maybe you need to lie down."

He angled a smile at her. "Is that an invitation?"

Her breath caught, but she snapped back, "In your dreams."

"How did you know?" He got up from the couch and came nearer, his breath becoming a soft wind on her face. Her heart pounded. She should go back to the sanctuary of the housekeeper's suite. But her feet stayed stubbornly glued to the carpet, and she didn't resist when Nate's good arm came around her, pulling her closer.

She'd never had much patience with intoxicated men, but this, *this* was different. She sensed the wine was his excuse for something he'd wanted to do all along.

His apparent unsteadiness didn't apply to his hold on her, she noticed. His grip was unyielding, his mouth barely inches above hers. When he kissed her, the intensity shook her. Like touching a live wire, she felt the impact all the way to the soles of her feet. Could she possibly look as dazed as she felt?

Evidently she could. When he drew his mouth away, his look seared her, the hunger in his gaze shocking and thrilling her. "Emma."

The whispered sound of her name should have brought her to her senses. Instead she felt herself going under and couldn't manage to fight the sensation. Rising onto her toes, she claimed his mouth, winding her arm around his neck to seal the kiss. Wildfire raged through her, pooling as heat deep inside.

He'd kissed her before but not with such demand. Her heartbeat triple-timed. Her breathing clogged. Speech froze. She simply took.

HE WAS ON FIRE. NATE KNEW he should stop before he frightened her off. Yet she didn't seem scared. She wound around him like strands of DNA, all eagerness, all softness. She made his body react in ways he wouldn't be able to control for much longer.

Blaming Troy was a cop-out. The jealousy gripping Nate was his alone. All Troy had done by his presence was make Nate face the truth. He didn't want a future with Emma, but he didn't want any other man having her, either. Seeing Troy flirting with her with his talk of trackside passes to watch him race had made Nate mad enough to do bodily harm.

So much for his Hippocratic oath.

Nor could he blame the wine for taking the edge off his caution. Around Emma, caution was history anyway. Despite all the reasons this wasn't a good idea, he wanted her. Wanted his fingers in her hair and her body molded against him. Wanted to lose himself in her. Where were two good hands when he needed them?

When she'd asked if he wanted to get back to work, he'd actually had to think about the answer. For as long as he could remember, he'd lived to perform surgery. But until now he'd never had anyone at home worth spending time with. Now there was Emma. And nowhere else he'd rather be.

The novelty rocked him, making him deepen the kiss. He heard her sharp intake of breath and felt her responses shimmy through her. When his tongue flicked over her lips, she parted them and he plunged.

She tasted of herbal tea, home-baked bread and woman. And sex. Hell. He lifted his head. There was no getting around his growing need to do more than kiss her. He wanted to touch her everywhere, lose himself inside her.

When she dropped her head back, he let his mouth roam greedily over the expanse of her throat and down to where the open buttons of her shirt revealed a tempting cleavage. As he explored, her breath caught and he felt her fingers scrape over his hair.

Needing more, he freed his arm from the sling and rested his splinted wrist against her nape while he slid his good hand inside her shirt, over tantalizing wisps of lace, until his fingers found their target. He kneaded and caressed, her lushness, her softness making his blood sing.

He was about to sweep her into his arms and carry her to the bed to continue where he'd left off yesterday, but stopped. He couldn't carry her anywhere.

Desire warred with a frustration so deep it felt like pain.

EMMA STARED AT HIM. "WHY DID you stop?"

He indicated the splint. "I'm not much good to you like this."

"You were doing fine."

"That was only a kiss."

There was nothing *only* about what he'd done to her. A kiss was the meeting of lips, the mingling of breath. His kiss was sex on a stick. "Didn't you say you could improvise?"

His dark look fired her blood. "You remember that?"

"Some things you don't forget." Her eyes gleamed. "Unless it was all talk."

A low protest started in his throat. "Who are you calling all talk?"

She lifted her palm to his cheek. "If the shoe fits…"

Turning his head, he nipped the fleshy heel of her hand. She dragged in a breath as raw need poured through her.

Through him, too, she saw. "Do you know what you do to me, Emma?"

"Rile you, resist you, second-guess you."

"All the above, but mainly drive me crazy." Desire glittered in his eyes. "I've never walked away from a challenge yet."

Is that what she was? Did she want to be loved by him as some unbeatable foe? What would be left once he'd claimed her? They'd be as far apart as ever. How could she live with the everyday, after he'd shown her paradise?

His lips roved over her face. "You're thinking again."

"I need to. Just…give me a moment." Almost impossible with her mind in such turmoil.

"If you have doubts…"

She pressed a finger to his lips, silencing him. "Not about this."

He nibbled the sensitive pads, eliciting another gasp. "Then what?"

"Us."

"I'm not asking for promises, Emma."

Nor was he offering any. But nobody said anything about mindless, showstopping sex. Could that work for her? Maybe it was the only thing that could.

"Yes," she said, her breath rushing out.

He didn't waste any more time on words, but used his good hand to push her shirt off her shoulders. She removed her bra and he bent to kiss her breasts. Burning with need, she eased her pants down her hips to pool on the floor.

His fingers feathered down her spine, eliciting a wave of tremors, then hooked inside the waist of her panties until he was cupping her behind, dragging her against his erection and making the blood thrum in her ears.

"I'll need help with my shirt," he said, his voice thickening.

Her hands shook as she undid the buttons and rested her palms against his chest. She fumbled with his belt buckle until she worked out the secret, then laughed.

"What's so funny?" he demanded.

"Is this what it's like for a man when he has to deal with a bra?"

He swatted her rear playfully. "Leading question. Let's see how you do with the zipper."

"You think I'm not up for the challenge?" Flicking her tongue to the corner of her mouth, she unzipped him and he kicked his pants aside. A scattering of hair teased her skin as, with calculated slowness, she helped him ease his shorts off, hearing him groan.

Desire ripped through her as he pulled her backward with him. He landed on the wide leather sofa with Emma on top. She saw his look of alarm. "Did I hurt your arm?"

As they fell he'd braced his splinted wrist along the sofa back. "My arm isn't the problem. If you keep moving, we won't get to second base."

A sense of power rushed through her. Deliberately she sat up, her knees on either side of his hips, and trailed her hands down his flanks as far as she could reach. He bucked, swore, steadied.

"You told me to improvise," she said primly.

"I didn't say you could kill me."

Her need for him was close to killing her. Passion drugged her, the power to excite him thrilled her. He was hers to command, but she was also his. Did he know? His dark gaze betrayed little, but the tension she felt in his muscles was more revealing. She leaned forward and kissed him.

It wasn't a kiss so much as a full-blown battering of her senses. At last he dragged his mouth away and moved lower to taste her breasts, insatiable, questing.

When he groped next to the sofa for his pants, she thought for a panicky moment he might be getting dressed, and everything in her screamed in denial. But he took a square of foil out of his wallet. "Before you say anything, this has been here for a while."

He wanted her to know this wasn't a habit, she thought, exultant that he felt the need to tell her.

Using his teeth, he ripped the foil open and handed the packet to her. Again, power thrilled through her as she wriggled down his thighs to sheathe him.

His back arched. "Now, Emma."

All instinct, she lifted herself to take him into her. But nothing prepared her for the onslaught of sensation as he drove deep inside her, sending her senses whirling.

USED TO BEING THE ONE IN control, Nate had to fight the urge to roll Emma over to finish what they'd started, but his wrist couldn't take the strain. He wasn't sure the rest of him could, either. She was driving him crazy, every touch sending his pulses into the stratosphere and his heart into an unsafe rhythm. But with her, he didn't want safety. He wanted, needed, to possess her. Now.

Her cry as he moved inside her almost made him

pause until he saw the wild-eyed pleasure in her expression. Her gaze went unfocused and she began to move with him, riding the peaks and valleys of desire like a surfer on a tumultuous ocean.

Slowly, slowly, he cautioned himself. Might as well have tried to hold back a raging tiger with his bare hands. With an effort, he made himself ease back and look at the sheer beauty of her poised over him, her lushness open to him like the fulfillment of a dream.

Her hair had come loose and flowed to her shoulders, over his hand like silk. He fisted his fingers through the mass, hearing her make a quiet sound of pleasure that echoed deep within him.

"Yes, Nate, yes."

The plea shattered his fragile control and he began to move again, began to share everything he was with her, taking everything she was in return.

The waves took them higher, roaring in his ears as he carried her with him, until, with a cry wrenched from deep inside, he brought them both crashing down. Panting, she lay across his chest, her skin sleek with heat. But he wasn't done yet.

Sliding his hand between them, he heard her catch her breath, then saw her eyes widen as his fingers went to work. The touch that could massage life back into a still heart worked its own kind of magic. He felt her heart drumming against his chest as the waves took her again, lifting her until she crested the last breaker on a mindless cry before collapsing into his embrace.

His eyelids drooped but he kept hold of her, not ready to abandon a closeness he'd never known he needed before Emma. No promises, he'd said. Who was he fooling? Her, he hoped. Certainly not himself.

He wanted and needed her, not only in his bed, but in his life. If she had the slightest clue, she'd be out of here in a heartbeat. And if he had any sense, he'd let her go.

This, whatever it was between them, was a one-way ticket to impossible. He couldn't give up medicine any more than he could willingly stop breathing. Like his mother, Emma wasn't prepared to be married to a doctor and he couldn't blame her. He'd seen how his mother suffered. How could he do that to a woman he…liked as much as Emma?

Why wasn't there some middle ground?

"Nate?"

Her soft voice punctured his thoughts. He found himself stroking her hair as she lay across his chest. "What?"

"This changes everything, doesn't it?"

With an effort, he made his tone light. "We don't want it to, do we?"

Her sigh whispered against him. "No."

She sounded about as convinced as he felt. He almost made the mistake of asking if she'd changed her mind about them, about a future together. Then realized the gentle purr he could hear was her. She had drifted off to sleep.

That was supposed to be his act. Yet he didn't feel sleepy. Sex as hard, fast and satisfying as this usually put him out like a light. Instead, his mind reeled. Careful not to disturb her, he pulled the throw from the back of the sofa over them both, angling his splinted wrist against his body. She moved slightly, her hair spilling over his hand, more soothing than any medication.

He looked down at her, wondering what the hell he was going to do about her.

THE INSISTENT RING TONE of Blondie's "Eat to the Beat" dragged Emma out of a delicious dream where she was entwined with a naked man, his arm clamped around her. Struggling to surface, she realized she was entwined…with Nate, and he was fast asleep. The memory of last night flooded back in mind-splintering detail.

Before her cell phone could wake him, she levered herself off the couch—and him. She grabbed his shirt, draping it around her as she located the phone in the kitchen.

It was Sophie and she sounded miserable. "I can't come to work today, Em. I have the migraine from hell."

"What time is it?"

"Just after six. Did I wake you?"

Through the open door of the den, Emma could see Nate on the sofa, the throw rug barely covering his magnificent body. She gulped air, remembering how his hardness had felt against her softness. "It's time I was awake." Joanna would be arriving at eight. The thought of how she might have found them made heat surge into Emma's face. "I'm sorry you're not well."

"Luckily we don't have much on today," Sophie said.

Emma pulled her thoughts together with an effort. "There's only the charity afternoon tea. Most of the baking's done and they're providing their own tea and coffee. It's an easy delivery, so I'll be fine." Professionally, anyway. Personally, she was a long way from certain. "Can I bring you anything?"

"If you're going by the office on your way, I'm pretty sure I left the prescription for my medication in the apron I forgot to take with me when we moved to Nate's kitchen."

"If it's there, I'll find it, get it filled and bring it over." Doug might be on site, but he'd told her he couldn't start the removal process until his team was available tomorrow.

"Thanks. I'm going to lie down again."

Emma smiled into the phone. "Confucius says Woman with headache sleeps alone."

She was gratified when Sophie laughed. "Ouch, even laughing hurts. I'll gladly sleep alone today."

Emma closed the phone and buttoned Nate's shirt, trying not to inhale the scent clinging to the expensive fabric. Trying not to relive her own foolishness. Before she drifted into sleep, he'd made it clear that last night would change nothing between them. Not that she expected it to. Wanting was another matter.

Once his injury healed, his work would reclaim him and there would be little room for her in his life. She'd known the risk when she let him make love to her. If she felt changed and he didn't, it was her own fault.

She put croissants in the oven to heat and was setting up the coffee machine when she heard him stirring. Her heart stirred in response. Cool, calm, she ordered herself. She kept her back to the door and busied herself with her task.

"That shirt looks a lot better on you than it does on me," he said, his voice husky.

Unable to stop herself, she looked around, almost blurting out her feelings at the sight of him framed in the doorway. His jeans were slung low over his hips, the belt undone and his broad chest was bare. Her fingers itched to touch, to taste, but look where that had gotten her. "Are you hungry? We didn't get around to dinner last night," she said, her throat infuriatingly dry.

He slanted her a grin. "We had better things to do."

She willed herself not to blush, a futile attempt as she felt color rush into her cheeks. "Coffee and croissants will be ready in a few minutes. Then I'll make an omelet."

He moved closer, dropping a kiss in the sensitive curve between her neck and shoulder. "I'll have a quick shower first. You?"

"In a little while," she said. "Nate, last night…"

"Was last night," he said firmly. "No strings, right?"

She could hardly argue with her own rules. "Of course not."

WHY DID NATE HAVE THE FEELING it wasn't what she'd wanted him to say? He was usually pretty good at reading people. Part of skilled doctoring was being able to assess a patient's general condition from their movements and demeanor as soon as they walked into the office. But Emma was a mass of contradictions. Impossible to read. One minute she wanted no part of his life, the next she erupted like a volcano in his arms. Which was the real Emma?

Keeping his injured arm clear, he turned the shower on full blast, relishing the cleansing stream. For a man who'd slept on a couch, he felt rested, strong. Better than he had for days. His wrist was improving, he found, as he wiggled his fingers. Soon he could start squeezing a rubber ball and using a keyboard to increase flexibility.

He grinned. He'd felt flexible enough last night. Seeing Emma in nothing but his shirt skimming her shapely thighs had him ready to test that flexibility again. But she'd looked conflicted. As if she couldn't decide how she felt about last night.

He'd tried to reassure her by saying that nothing had changed between them. Unless…he clicked off the shower and grabbed a towel, winding it around his hips. Unless she'd wanted things to change.

Now there was a thought.

## CHAPTER FOURTEEN

EMMA SHOULD FEEL PLEASED with her day. After adding the finishing touches to the menu, she'd delivered the order to the children's charity hosting the afternoon tea for their committee. The response couldn't have been more positive. Next stop was her place to look for Sophie's prescription.

Emma parked outside the house. No hazard warning signs yet, although most of the work would take place at the back. The building felt chilly as she let herself in the front door.

Some of the chill was inside her. Yesterday she'd known who she was, and what she wanted. Last night Nate had awakened feelings and stirred needs she'd thought long banished. Apparently they were only on her side.

Over breakfast he'd been so matter-of-fact she wanted to scream. But she'd made polite conversation as if last night hadn't happened. As if he hadn't possessed both her willing body and her less willing mind.

He'd offered to write Sophie a prescription for her meds to save Emma the trip. "It's on my way," she'd said, not wanting favors from him. Not wanting anything, except possibly a repeat of the nirvana she'd found in his arms last night. Not going to happen, she assured herself. The foundations of her existence felt rocky enough as it was.

Sophie's apron hung on a hook in the hallway, the prescription still in the pocket. Tucking the piece of paper into her bag, Emma went into the shell of her kitchen. The contents were stacked in the front room and some of the floorboards were up.

Placing her bag near the wall, Emma looked down, her eyes widening. Under her feet was a brick-lined room that might have been a cellar until access was sealed off. She hadn't known the space existed.

A pile of clothing and what looked like years of debris cluttered the cellar floor. A rickety set of steps led down into the gloom but started well below the kitchen floor level. She shuddered. Confined spaces made her anxious. Even if the steps could hold her, she didn't plan on exploring.

Then she heard the sound.

Mice? Surely not rats? The building was treated regularly against pests. Sophie said she thought the place was haunted. Could she be right?

Intending to get out as fast as possible, Emma hesitated. If someone was in trouble down there, could she walk away? She didn't believe in ghosts. More likely someone's pet was trapped under the cellar floor. Before she could change her mind, she groped with her feet for the steps, testing them before releasing her grip on the edge of the hole and climbing down.

Actually, climbing was a stretch. The reality was more of a controlled fall. The cellar was deeper than it looked from above, and by the time her feet touched solid ground, her breath was pumping. She wiped her clammy hands on her shirt. From the look of the splintered steps, they weren't good for a return climb.

Panic threatened until she looked at the patch of light above. She was safe. She could pile up some of the junk to help her get out. And Nate knew where she was. If she didn't show up at his home, he'd come looking. The thought of him calmed her.

"Is anyone down here?" she called, hearing her voice tremble

What she'd taken for a pile of rags in the corner moved slightly. She dropped to her knees. "Doug? Oh, God, what happened?"

He must have fallen or collapsed into the cellar, landing on his back, the debris breaking his fall. She shook him gently then tapped his cheeks. "Doug, can you hear me?"

No response. Damn. She couldn't call for an ambulance because her phone was in the kitchen above, well out of reach. Helplessness gripped her. She fought it. She wasn't four years old anymore.

*Focus. Doug needs help. Think about him, not yourself.*

How could she, when she was as trapped as he was? The urge to curl up into a shivering ball alarmed her. Blackness ringed her vision. She was spinning off into a nightmare she couldn't make go away.

A dream of being trapped underground had haunted her for years. Now she was living the fear. Reason threatened to desert her.

*No.* She couldn't give in. Doug's life might depend on her ability to function. She had to keep a grip. What would Nate do?

Slowly, the first-aid lessons she'd taken years ago started to come back to her. Doug was already lying on his back. When she checked, she could find no sign of broken bones. Had he fallen in or collapsed down here?

*Doesn't matter. Make sure he can breathe.*

With two fingers she lifted his chin and pushed down on his forehead with her other hand. She couldn't see his chest move, and when she placed her ear next to his mouth and nose, she felt no breath on her cheek.

*OhGodohGodohGod.*

"Emma!"

Dazedly she looked up. Had she conjured Nate up out of fear and desperation? He couldn't possibly be here. But he was, crouched at the edge of the hole above her head. Doug must have left the back door unlocked when he arrived, and been checking things out when he fell. None of that explained what Nate was doing here.

"Nate, it's Doug. He's unconscious and not breathing."

He must have heard the panic in her voice. "It's going to be all right. Did you see him collapse?"

"No, but he moved slightly when I climbed down. His breathing must have only just stopped."

"Here's what I want you to do."

"Can't you help him?" Again, she cursed the child-like voice that had somehow replaced her own.

"I can't get down to you with only one hand. You can do this, sweetheart."

Wonderful, calm voice. Some of her panic ebbed. *Sweetheart? Mustn't think about that now.* "We're in good hands," she said to the unconscious builder, then raised her voice. "What…what do I do?"

"Keep Doug's chin lifted and head tilted. Pinch his nose closed and cover his mouth with yours. Give him two slow, full breaths."

Her breaths gasped out, sounding loud to her own ears. "That's good," Nate said in the same steady tone. "Your breath is probably high in $CO_2$. That'll start his chemoreceptors working faster."

His tone suggested that was a positive thing. At his command, she gave two more breaths. "He's still not breathing."

"Okay, peel back his eyelid and tell me what you see."

"His pupil…it's contracted."

"Good, that's good. Now find the sternum, the breastbone, right between the nipples. You need to be over the lower part of the sternum. You don't want to bruise the liver or damage a rib."

*OhGodohGod.* "I'm there," she said, forcing herself to sound calm.

As Nate leaned down to check her position, his shadow darkened the space, making fear claw at her throat. *Not now. There isn't time.* She made herself concentrate on Nate's voice.

"Perfect. Make a tightly clenched fist and thump as hard as you can on the sternum from about a hand span away, then pull your hand clear."

"I wish you were doing this." With a quick prayer, she followed his orders and was stunned by the instant reaction. "He's started breathing. I can't believe it, he's actually breathing."

Nate must have heard Doug cough. "We call that a precordial thump. Gets the heart going again six times out of ten."

The walls felt as if they were pressing in on her. *Breathe. Breathe.* Was she telling herself or Doug? "What next?"

"I've called an ambulance. Keep an eye on Doug and tell me if he stops breathing again."

The contractor gave a low groan. "I think he's coming around."

"That's normal, too. He'll be on his way to the hospital soon."

She relayed Nate's comment. Doug nodded. He looked dazed and complained of being cold. "Better for your heart," Nate said, picking up on the question.

"Was…looking around…down here. Felt…massive pain…" Doug lifted a shaky hand to indicate his heart. Hardly aware of what she was saying, she began to talk about his discovery of the cellar and what it might be used for. Anything to keep him calm.

After what seemed like an age, Nate disappeared from sight. Panic assailed her again until she heard him talking to what must be the paramedics. The jargon was lost on her but it didn't matter. A uniformed man was lowering a ladder and jumping into the space to take over Doug's care. "You okay?" he asked as he passed her. "You're very pale."

"I don't like dark spaces. I'll be fine."

As she started to climb, Nate reached out his good hand to her. "Can you manage the ladder?"

"A lot easier than staying down here." Nate's grip felt strong as he helped her back into the light. When her legs threatened to give out, he hooked his arm around her. "You're in the wrong profession."

When her shaken look met his, he added, "Don't

take that the wrong way. I simply meant you performed as well as any med student I've ever seen."

For a minute, she'd thought…had this encounter almost blinded her to the gulf between them? But… *sweetheart?* "I feel dizzy," she said, putting a hand to her eyes.

He steered her to a substantial steel toolbox she hadn't noticed when she arrived. It must be Doug's. Her legs folded and she sat, listening to the activity in the cellar. "Will Doug be all right?" she asked when she could trust her voice again.

"In the hospital he'll be checked for any arterial blockages, treated with blood thinners or beta blockers, whatever he needs. But yes, his prognosis is excellent, thanks to you."

He blurred in her gaze. "I just did what you told me."

"That precordial thump is only taught to medical professionals, not in first-aid courses," he pointed out. "You performed like an expert."

"But I felt so helpless."

He went to cross his arms, remembered he couldn't, and braced his left hand on his hip. "Now you know."

"Know what?" Realization flooded through her. "This is what it's like for you, isn't it? For my parents and my brother. Grace. All of you. Dealing with life and death on a daily basis."

He nodded, his eyes bright. "The fear that you won't be able to help is always there."

"How do you stand the uncertainty?"

"You never stop learning," he said. "About your patients and about yourself. It's the only thing keeping the fear at bay."

Could her judgment be so flawed? How could she not have seen what they went through, every day, Nate, her parents and their parents? The worst she had to handle was a botched recipe or a faulty ingredient.

He read her so easily. "Now don't start in on yourself. Saving a life is possibly the most extraordinary experience a person can have, only matched by bringing a new life into the world. But there are other levels of helping and caring, and they're all valuable. This isn't a competition."

How could he think so? She felt like the last runner in an incredible race, where trying her hardest would never be enough.

He offered her his hand. "You're exhausted. We'll take a cab home. You're in no shape to drive."

"But the rental car…"

"Sophie can bring it back tomorrow if she's feeling better," he suggested.

"I found her prescription. She needs her medication."

"We'll have the cab stop by a pharmacy and get

the script filled, then drop it off to her on the way home."

Another question drove through her exhaustion. "Nate, what are you doing here?"

"Checking on you."

Before she could ask what he meant, the paramedics lowered a stretcher into the cellar. Shortly after, they lifted Doug out. The builder looked haggard, but smiled as he was carried past Emma. "Thanks," he murmured. "You, too, Doc. Next time I go exploring, I'll take one of you with me."

"I'm glad we were able to help," she said, feeling her heart swell.

Why was Nate still holding her hand? "Don't you want to go with him, make sure he's all right?"

"He's in great hands, and the hospital will contact his family. He'll have all the help he needs," he said. "You're my priority."

Had anyone ever said that to her before? If so, she couldn't remember when. Without warning, bile rose in her throat. Nate saw the color leave her face and got her to her feet, supporting her to the bathroom, where she emptied her stomach in a hideous rush. Then he sat her on the edge of the bath and sponged her face with a damp washcloth. "I'm s-sorry," she said through chattering teeth.

"It's only reaction," he assured her. "You held together when it counted."

Amazed that he didn't find her weakness a turnoff,

she dragged in a few breaths to calm herself. She still didn't know why Nate was really here. Checking on her, he'd said. Because he thought she needed help, or because he cared about her? He'd agreed not to interfere without asking her first, so how was she to read this?

With her nerves wire-taut and her legs barely holding her up, the time wasn't right for puzzles. And he was a puzzle. The longer she knew him, the less she understood him. Sophie believed male and female brains were differently wired. Being around Nate seemed to bolster the argument. Or maybe he was only being Nate.

He stood beside her as if ready to catch her if she fell. There was comfort in that, too. "Time to go home?" he asked.

She nodded, so eager to get out of there that it took a second to realize she did think of his place as home. Later she would examine what that meant. After the fear of being in the cellar, she craved space and light. The cab to take her to Nate's house couldn't get there quickly enough.

WHEN SHE FOUND OUT WHAT HE'D done, Emma was going to be furious, Nate thought. But he'd wanted her family to know she'd saved a man's life today. They were ready enough to criticize her. Time they cheered her heroism.

He'd spoken to Cherie between her patient appointments, and had practically heard her eyebrows lift when he told her. She'd said she couldn't talk to her daughter then, but that she'd come and see her tomorrow. Nate intended to hold her to the promise.

Ignoring Cherie's evident impatience with the discussion, he asked why Emma found confined, dark spaces so distressing. "She handled the CPR like a veteran, but by the time she got out of the cellar, she was almost on the point of collapse."

"We've never had a cellar or anything similar," Cherie said, sounding puzzled. "As a child, she hated going through tunnels and games like hide-and-seek, but I don't know why."

In some ways, Cherie knew less about Emma than he did. "As a clinician, you'd have found her reaction worrying if you'd seen it," he pointed out.

"Hmm. I'll talk to Greg tonight and see if he has any clues." With that, Nate had to be content.

No wonder Emma struggled with her family. Cherie had sounded as if Emma's bravery was only to be expected. And surely this wasn't the first time she'd shown symptoms of a full-blown phobia? Weren't any of them concerned about her? Nate sure as hell was. This time he couldn't kid himself his interest was medical.

He hadn't wanted to feel so strongly about Emma, but there were some things a man couldn't fight. Such as a woman getting under his skin as surely as if she'd inserted a central IV line directly to his heart.

At least he was man enough to put Emma's feelings first. She didn't want to be involved with anyone in his profession, and his own family experience made it easy to understand her reasons. It didn't stop him from trying to help her, though.

From Grace, he was aware of the gossip doing the rounds of the hospital about Emma sharing his house. He wouldn't be surprised if Cherie was fueling some of it. Not that he minded as much as he might have once. Having his name coupled with Emma's was starting to feel alarmingly comfortable.

Like the way she looked now, asleep in her bed in the housekeeper's suite.

Comfortable and about eighteen, he decided. An improvement on her near panic and nausea earlier. He had to resist the urge to smooth the hair away from her face as she slept.

He'd found it tough enough keeping his hands to himself while she showered and changed. For once, he'd managed the kitchen, insisting she take things easy. Okay, with one hand, he could only heat up the frittata she'd prepared yesterday, and put together a basic salad, but she'd reacted as if he'd done something remarkable. He'd felt ten feet tall.

She had a knack for appreciating small things. When he'd been with Pamela, two dozen roses were barely enough. With Emma, he had a feeling a single perfect bloom would send her into raptures. He made a mental note to test the theory soon.

Seeing his home through her eyes was also an education. The kitchen he'd rarely used was turning into a place of warmth while he watched. Meals he'd have eaten without noticing were now savored. He'd read a quote from Aldous Huxley that most human beings had an almost infinite capacity for taking things for granted. Emma turned that notion completely on its head. Brave new world, indeed.

He'd meant to tell her he'd spoken to her mother, but hadn't been able to bring himself to spoil the mood. By bedtime, he still hadn't said anything, telling himself she'd been through enough for one day. When he'd offered her his room, wanting no more than to keep a medical eye on her, she'd insisted she was fine in the housekeeper's suite but had agreed to let him look in on her once she was changed and in bed.

When he did, he saw that the suite was more homey with her things scattered around. After a matter of days the rooms looked lived-in, the decorator accessories mingling with a couple of scented candles, a kookaburra soft toy and some hair doodads.

Exhausted, she must have fallen asleep almost immediately. Her hair was down now, falling across the pillow. In the glow of a night-light, the strands shone red-gold, making him want to bury his face in their softness. Instead, he settled his head back against the recliner chair, stretched his long legs in front of him, and simply watched.

EMMA WAS RUNNING, THE LOW-hanging branches slapping her as she tore through them. Her breathing was loud and her heart almost bumped out of her chest. The sound was nearly as loud as when her father had let her listen to her heartbeat through his stethoscope.

Instinct told her the harder she ran, the closer she'd get to Gramma Jessie's house. Except she couldn't see the house through the thick bush, and all she could hear was the creek running over rocks. Stumbling, she noticed a patch of red flowers. They were the only red flowers she'd seen, and there was the big black rock behind them. She was running in circles, not getting closer to home, but more and more lost.

A sob erupted from her throat but she pushed it back. Daddy said big girls didn't cry. They thought about what they needed to do, and then did it. But he hadn't been lost in the bush, chased by an angry bee because she'd picked the wild flower he was feeding on. She hadn't meant to take his flower, but the bee wouldn't stop chasing her.

Suddenly the earth gave way underneath her. A huge tree had fallen over, leaving a hole where its roots had been torn out of the ground. She tried to slow her headlong rush, but her feet slipped and she slid down, down, down until she landed at the bottom of the hole, all the breath rushing out of her. Soil rained down around her, over her clothes and hair. If it didn't stop, they'd never find her. She clawed at the soft earth, screaming for her father as the blackness threatened to swallow her up.

"EMMA, WAKE UP. YOU'RE SAFE."

She fought as hard as she could against the tree roots tangling around her, then slowly realized where she was. The roots were strong male arms holding her, making her feel secure. "Nate?"

He nodded. "You were having a nightmare."

"Did I wake you?" She must have been loud enough to bring him from the other side of the house.

"I wasn't far away."

Then her vision cleared and she saw the still-rocking chair and the blanket he'd tossed aside in his haste to get to her. "You've been here all night?"

"I was worried. You did so well with Doug, then fell apart."

She tried for lightness. "Story of my life."

His hold tightened. "I don't buy that, and neither should you. You're a strong woman, Emma. Stronger than you know."

Her voice felt strangled. "How can you say that?" All her life she'd been told what she couldn't do. How could Nate have such faith in her? She tried to identify what else she could see shining in his eyes, and resisted putting it into words. Afraid to be wrong.

"Easily. Doug Armstrong is alive today because you faced your greatest fear to save him."

Still feeling the effects of the nightmare, she tried to see what he was getting at. "Fear? I don't understand."

Nate ran his hand over her tangled hair. "I suspect this fear goes much deeper. Tell me what you remember from your nightmare."

## CHAPTER FIFTEEN

EMMA FELT HER JAW SET. "Not much. It was only a bad dream."

"Then tell me the bits you do remember."

He was taking her seriously, she thought, and her emotions were raw enough that for once, just once, she felt safe sharing the dream with another person. No censure lurked in Nate's gaze. No surface reassurance. But no letting her dismiss her experience as unimportant, either. "I was afraid. Terribly, terribly frightened."

As her breath quickened, she felt him massage the small of her back, the circular movements sure and comforting through her nightdress. And arousing enough that she wanted to pull his head down and draw his mouth close enough to kiss.

He wasn't going to be sidetracked, though. "Frightened of what?"

"That's just it, I don't know. I knew when I was in the dream, but like always, when I woke up the details vanished."

"You've had this dream before?"

"On and off for years. Not recently, though."

He frowned. "Until something triggered it again. You were in the cellar with Doug, it was dark, confined, probably felt damp—"

"Don't," she cut in, her voice hoarse. "You're not my doctor."

"Just as well, since I'm your lover," he said.

"We made love. It's not the same." She wouldn't let it be the same.

His expression darkened. Now what? "I won't push if you don't want me to. But I think you do. And one thing about us doctors, we're good at keeping secrets."

"No," she protested sharply. "I don't like secrets."

"Is this dream about a secret, Emma?"

She tried to push him away but he held fast. At the mention of secrets, her expression had gone blank and when she spoke, her voice sounded as if she was back in the dream of being four years old, confirmed when she said, "Yes….no. Daddy said we should keep this a secret."

*Oh, God, no.* Nate felt dread ram a fist down his throat. "Why, Emma?"

"He didn't want my mother to worry."

"That was long ago. You can tell the secret now. Your mother would want to know." He prayed he was telling the truth.

Emma's beautiful face had become masklike, confirming his suspicion that she was reliving the event in her mind. "I wasn't supposed to wander off. I was picking flowers for Gramma Jessie. She likes flowers. There was a bee in one. I dropped the flower but he chased me all the way to the creek."

This wasn't what he'd expected to hear. "What happened then?"

"I got lost. Really, really lost. Then I fell in the hole where the tree toppled over after the storm yesterday. It left this big dark, damp hole taller than me." Her voice wavered, fell silent.

He shook her gently to bring her out of the memory. "Emma, sweetheart, this wasn't yesterday. You remembered something you went through a long time ago. It's in the past and can't hurt you now."

She gave her head a little shake. The mask was replaced by an expression so open, so vulnerable that his heart ached. Was he the first to hear this story? The level of trust that implied blew his mind. At the same time, he felt relief at seeing her become fully aware of he surroundings again. "Do you remember what happened after you fell in that hole?"

"Dirt showered down on me." Her voice sounded steadier. "I couldn't climb out. I thought I was going to be buried."

Being buried alive was a fear so primal, people had placed breathing devices in coffins just in case. He suppressed a shudder. "What happened then?"

"I don't know. Wait. Yes, I do. I started singing to calm myself."

The thought of Emma as a little girl, suffering that way, made him want to rip an unfeeling universe apart with his hands. "You were strong even then, sweetheart."

She gave him a rueful look. "My father didn't think so. He heard me and pulled me out, then told me off for getting lost. He didn't want to hear about the bee."

Nate wanted to shout with relief. It wasn't what he'd feared after all. "He was probably out of his mind with worry. Parents of lost kids often say they'll hug the child first, then threaten what they'll do to them if they ever run off again."

Her smile turned wistful. "I think my dad forgot the hugging part."

Nate made up for it now, clamping her against his chest as if he never intended to let her go. He felt her heart beating against him, lovely, strong heartbeat. Lovely, strong woman. While he still could, he released his hold, but kept an arm around her. "Are you sure?"

"About the hugging? I don't know. I mostly remember the yelling and how cold and angry he was. He insisted that I shouldn't tell my mother what happened."

"Did he explain why?"

"He said it would be our secret so my mother wouldn't get upset with me for going near the creek. Until now, I'd forgotten about falling in the hole."

"You repressed the memory," Nate said. "But it surfaced in your dream tonight. When you got out of the cellar, you were almost in shock, so I knew something else was affecting you."

"I'm sorry for making such a fool of myself."

"Don't," he snapped, his tone bringing her head up. "Don't apologize for being human. Courage isn't rushing headlong into danger. It's being afraid and doing what you have to do anyway. By that reckoning, you're a true hero."

Emma felt as if a huge burden had been lifted from her shoulders. Knowing why she hated dark places might not remove the fear, but understanding was a start. "Thank you," she said softly.

She let herself reach up and find his mouth as she'd wanted to do since she awoke. The instant her lips met his, it set off a chain reaction of yearning.

With the bedcovers layered between them, body contact was limited, but she felt his muscles tighten as she pressed closer. His hand pulled her against the hardness of his chest. Nightmares and fears dissolved into needs and desires.

When he tried to stroke her hair with his splinted hand, she heard his throaty sound of frustration. To help, she linked her hands around his neck, clinging so he didn't have to support her, freeing his good hand to cup her nape. The sensation was unbelievable.

"Your hair smells wonderful," he murmured, burying his face against her neck. "Like a garden."

"My shampoo," she said. He kissed the hollow at her nape and along her collarbone. He probably knew the clinical name for every bone in her body. All she knew was that bones could melt when kissed.

She was well into the melting stage when he pulled away.

He gathered himself with visible effort. "You're not up to this."

Disappointment shivered through her. "I thought we agreed you aren't my doctor."

"But I do care about you."

Not in the way she wanted him to, apparently. She resisted the urge to pull the bedcovers prudishly around her, and cloaked herself in dignity instead. "And you don't like the feeling."

"I like it well enough."

His guarded tone chilled her. "Then what's the problem?"

Levering himself to his feet, he began to pace. "You're the problem. We're both the problem for each other." He swung around. "You've told me often enough you don't want to get involved with a doctor."

Hard to see how she could get any more deeply involved. "Are you trying to say you have regrets?"

"Of course I do. Not about making love to you. Never that."

"Then what?"

He gestured around them. "Dragging you into my

life. I saw what being married to a doctor did to my mother. I won't do that to you."

"You don't have to. Things can change." Who was she trying to convince?

"I'm an all-or-nothing man. There isn't room for anything besides my career."

"Nate, that might have been true once. But you've already changed. When you were told you could return to surgery in another couple of weeks, you looked…I don't know…disappointed."

"I admit I wasn't as thrilled about the prospect as I thought I'd be."

"Do you know why?" When he looked as if he was about to protest, she held up her hands. "Fair's fair. You had your turn digging around in my psyche."

"No hidden secrets, no surprises. What you see is what you get."

"Except I don't *get* anything."

"It's nearly daylight; Joanna will be arriving soon."

"Oh, you fight dirty, Dr. Hale. What if I told you I don't care if she finds us in bed together?" Emma was surprised to discover it was the truth.

He released her hands from his neck, kissing her fingers before he stood up, causing her heart to give a slight skip. "I believe you, but it isn't that simple. Your parents are coming to see you this morning."

"They're coming here? Why?"

"I told them what happened yesterday."

Her heart jolted, then anger flooded through her. "You shouldn't have, Nate. It's not as if I was hurt or anything."

She flung the covers away to see that her nightgown had ridden up. His gaze heated at the sight of her long legs. "When will you stop deciding what's good for me?"

"Would you have told them yourself?"

She dragged a robe from the foot of the bed and jerkily pushed her arms into the sleeves. "Eventually."

He angled one shoulder against the door frame. "I thought it was time they heard something good about their daughter."

"I can imagine my mother's excitement."

His eyes narrowed. "She's relieved you're okay. And impressed that you saved Doug's life."

Emma couldn't mask the flicker of hope. "Really?" When Nate didn't answer right away, she dropped her gaze. "That's what I thought."

"They want the best for you," he suggested.

She gathered her hair off her neck and secured the twist with a clip. "Their definition of *best* is me marrying a doctor so I fit into their world…your world."

"A moment ago, you didn't think that was such a bad idea."

"Nobody said anything about marrying. A moment ago, I wanted you to make love to me."

"And now?"

"I still want you to." *Did he have any idea how much?* "But you've invited my parents over, so the question is moot."

"What does *moot* mean, anyway?"

Her eyes snapped. "In this case, it means impractical. I'm not going to be having sex when my parents arrive."

"Then we're taking a rain check?"

Mindful of his wrist, she gave him a gentle but firm push. "You're getting out of here while I shower and dress, then I'll make breakfast."

Once again he surprised her by having the table set and French toast sizzling when she joined him in the kitchen. "How did you manage one-handed?"

"I talked Joanna through making the egg mixture last night, so I only had to soak the sliced bread and toss it into a pan. Electric can opener took care of the berries, which I'm warming. All you have to do is sit down at the table and eat."

Unused to being waited on, Emma played with the cutlery. Villeroy & Boch, like the dinnerware, she noticed idly. Must be a favorite of Nate's. Unless his decorator had made the choice for him. How did you read a man without clues to his personal tastes? The lack of clues were in themselves clues, she decided, resting her chin on her hand. Nate didn't have time to decorate his own home. How much time would he have for love when a partner couldn't be outsourced like so much of his life? Everything besides medicine. *And why do I care?*

Confusion rolled through her. He was in a kitchen he barely knew his way around, cooking a meal for her. He was either still in medical mode and considering her well-being, or she meant something to him. He was certainly starting to mean more to her, she acknowledged, pensively twirling a fork. Letting him think she only wanted sex wasn't wholly honest. She wanted him, period. Waking up to him this morning had felt so right.

*Oh, Ma, you would be planning the wedding if you could hear me thinking.* The idea wasn't as impossible as Emma had once believed. She could actually imagine herself walking down the aisle toward Nate.

Get real, she ordered herself. He didn't want the commitment, and she was dreaming if she thought life with Nate would be different from growing up in her family. He'd said himself he didn't want them to end up like his parents, driven apart by work pressures. Why wasn't her heart paying attention?

Nate was the injured one; she'd been hired to feed him. She jumped to her feet, determined to set him straight on their relationship, but he was coming through the door carrying a plate. "I'll be back with mine," he said, putting the plate in front of her.

She couldn't help it. She gaped. He'd not only cooked the French toast to puffy perfection, but dusted it with sugar and mounded the drained berries carefully between the slices. Good grief, he'd even spotted drops of strawberry syrup around the edge of the plate by way of presentation.

With a bump, she sat down. "Where did you learn to do this?" she asked when he returned with his plate.

"I worked my way through medical school as a barista in a café."

Now she knew why he made good coffee. "But the food presentation?"

"Observation is a key skill in medicine. I watched and learned."

"But you never cook."

"What's the point when I'm only making dinner for one? Eat before this gets cold."

She ate. The creamy French toast contrasted deliciously with the tartness of the unsweetened berries. "This is good," she said around a mouthful.

He reached across the table and dabbed at the corner of her mouth with a napkin. "Berry juice. Do you still think I'm a one-trick pony?"

"I'm sure you have others, but don't choose to use them." She gestured with her fork. "This for example. You have the makings of a passable cook."

"Only passable?"

"Way better. I might try you on the spinach roulade I'm preparing as part of an order for tonight."

His eyes sparkled. "I might surprise you."

Surprising her was becoming routine. She had to be careful he didn't surprise her into making an admission he didn't want to hear. That she was falling in love with him. Shock made the fork slip, landing with a crash onto the plate.

He was beside her in seconds, his cool fingers dropping to her wrist. "I'm okay," she insisted, his touch vibrating through her.

"Are you sure? You went pale and your pulse is a little fast."

Realizing you were in love would do that.

SOPHIE HAD GONE TO PICK UP some ingredients they needed. Emma was well into preparations for the cocktail party they were catering when Nate's doorbell chimed. Not close enough to the video monitor to see who the caller was, she tensed at the sound of her father's voice as Joanna showed him in.

She washed her hands and untied her apron, then went into the den. Nate stood beside the fireplace and Greg Jarrett sat beside her mother on the sofa. A tall, rangy man who looked more like a farmer than a senior obstetrician, he seemed ill at ease. Which made two of them, she thought as she took a straight-backed chair. "What's this about, Ma?"

"Nate told us what happened yesterday. We wanted to be sure you're all right."

She flashed a look at Nate. "He should have told you I'm fine. So is Doug Armstrong." She'd called the hospital earlier, relieved to be told the builder was expected to fully recover.

"Thanks to you," her father observed. Then he frowned. "Nate said you had a phobic response to being in the cellar."

Again she glanced at Nate, this time in annoyance. "Nate fusses."

"With good cause," Cherie contributed. "Tell her, Greg."

Her father gathered himself with an effort. "It's my fault that you have a problem."

This was news. "This morning I remembered falling into the hole left by a tree at Gramma's place. Or I thought I had."

Her father linked his hands together. "Your memory is accurate. I planted the idea that you'd been playing by the creek, so you wouldn't tell your mother you'd been half-buried in that hole."

A memory of soil raining down on her flashed through her mind and she shuddered. "Why didn't you want me to remember?"

Her mother's face had gone pale. "He did it for my sake. You know that my parents met in a war zone?"

None of this was making much sense. "Yes. But what does that have to do with me?"

Her mother balked but Emma's father clasped her hand. "It's time she heard the whole story, Cherie. I'll tell her if you'd rather not."

Cherie shook her head. "My parents went through some really rough times in Vietnam. I was only thirteen when they took me to Ho Chi Minh City to show me where they'd met. We went on a tour into the countryside outside the city to see the networks of tunnels my parents said the Vietcong had used for surprise attacks."

Emma nodded. "I've heard of them. Grandma and Grandpa Kenner had to treat soldiers who'd gone into the tunnels and been maimed by booby traps or bitten by snakes and scorpions."

"Must have been disturbing for you as a teenager, Cherie," Nate contributed.

Greg looked down. "Worse than that. The ground was damp and she slipped and fell into one of the hidden air vents servicing the tunnels. She was trapped for hours before she could be freed."

Cherie nodded. "Your father didn't want to remind me of the horror of that day by telling me what had happened to you, Emma."

Greg lifted his gaze to Emma. "I owe you an apology for putting your mother's welfare before yours. Encouraging you to talk about what happened would have helped you process your fears and perhaps headed off a phobia."

"If I'd known, I might have been able to help you in some way," Cherie said.

When Emma sat in stunned silence, her father added, "Sorry is inadequate now, but it's all I can say, and I am truly sorry I let my career come between us. I thought you were doing okay, but I see now your experience did more harm than I realized."

More than he could imagine, she thought. She didn't kid herself he would change, or that her mother and brother would be less career focused. But she felt relieved at knowing what had happened. And her father's apology put them on a more even footing than she'd ever experienced.

Greg stood. "I'm glad Cherie knows the truth at last." He made a wry face. "When she told me about Nate's call and your reaction to being in the cellar, I told her everything."

"And I gave him hell for keeping it from me," Cherie said. "I'm a pediatrician. I should have been able to help my own daughter."

Compassion gripped Emma as her mother's voice cracked. She'd never heard Cherie sounding less than calm and capable. "I survived," Emma assured her shakily. Contrarily, she wanted her old mother back, and acknowledged how much comfort she had always drawn from Cherie's confidence. "You didn't know."

"I suspected something might be troubling you, but we were always too busy to delve. I hope you'll come to dinner tonight so we can start making amends."

"I'm working tonight." Seeing her father's face fall, she added, "But I'm free tomorrow. Nate might have other plans." She cursed the yearning she couldn't keep out of her voice.

She'd long thought of her father as a big man, but Nate was bigger, stronger, more masculine as he came to stand beside her. "Before you go, I have something to ask you."

A medical question about her, she supposed. Her stomach knotted in protest. "You don't have to, Nate."

His gaze swept over her, his expression unreadable. "I think I do. It might be old-fashioned, but I want to ask your parents for their blessing so we can get married."

"What?" Her knees weakened and he put his arm around her. "What did you say?"

Something like gratitude came into her father's face as he looked at Nate and smiled. "Patient's hearing is affected. Might be worth looking into."

"I'm not your patient, either of you," Emma protested. "And my hearing's fine."

Nate shrugged. "Emma thinks I meddle."

She struggled free and planted her hands on her hips. "What do you call this? Asking my parents if I want to marry you before you've asked me."

"Do you?"

"Of course I do." The admission slipped out. "I mean, I need to think about this. My business will be affected." *Not to mention the rest of her life.*

"So will mine," Nate said easily. "I can cope if you can."

Everything she'd seen so far suggested he could. But could she?

Her father moved toward her awkwardly, as if he wasn't sure what to do next. She made it easy for him by holding out her arms and he came into them. Forgiveness would take time, but Emma didn't believe in holding on to past grudges. Not when the future was so bright with promise. "What do you think, Dad?"

She saw something she'd never expected to see in her reserved father's eyes. A wet glimmer. "You're old enough to know your own mind, but for myself, I'm delighted."

"Me, too," Cherie agreed, sounding a little more like herself.

Nate stepped forward. "Thanks, Greg and Cherie. I'll take good care of your daughter."

Emma was tempted to stamp her foot, but she resisted. "I don't need taking care of, thank you very much."

Greg's hold tightened then he released her, looking older than she had ever seen him. "We'd better leave you two to work out the details."

"Yes." No sense fighting the inevitable. Emma saw her parents to the door and returned to find Nate looking so smug she wanted to smack him. "You realize you'll have to marry me after this? Knowing my mother, the news will be all over the hospital by lunchtime."

"Saves us telling everyone."

Already suspecting the answer, Emma asked anyway. "What happened to not wanting to put me through the same heartache your mother had with your father?"

"I still don't, and I won't. Spending the night watching you sleep, and holding you when you woke from the nightmare made me realize I can't let you go, so it's up to me to make sure my work never comes between us. My father never learned that lesson, but I will."

By now she knew him well enough to trust he meant what he said. "About the meddling in my life," she began.

"I can't promise not to meddle. It's inbred. But I'll try and remember to ask first."

She lifted a hand to his face. "As long as you try."

He released his breath. "It's all any of us can do, Emma. Mistakes are human and humans are often mistaken."

"Sounds like something Sophie would credit to Confucius."

"She's a smart woman."

Before Emma could agree, she found her words stolen by the pressure of his mouth.

None of this made any sense. All her life she'd

promised herself never to get involved with a doctor. But this was different. This was Nate.

"I can hear you thinking again," he said, his lips moving over her hairline and sending shivers of sensation down her spine.

"There's a lot to think about. This morning I woke up with no plans except organizing tonight's job, and now I'm discussing marriage with you."

"What else is there to discuss?"

"You haven't even asked me properly."

He held her a little away from him. "You want me to do the bended knee thing?"

With his injured hand, he'd have trouble. "No," she conceded. "You asked and I answered, however indirect it was. I guess it's a proposal to tell our children about in the future."

"Do you want children, Emma?"

She knew a second of concern. "Don't you?"

"They could turn out like Luke, lost and troubled."

"Or like you, brilliant and reliable to a fault."

He nodded. "Or some mix of us both we can't imagine yet."

A recipe for the future, she thought, banding her hands around the strong column of his neck. The day she'd stepped into his kitchen, she knew her life had changed. Now it was going to change again, in ways she couldn't fathom. She only knew she wanted this, wanted him, as she'd never wanted anything in her life. A sigh slipped between her lips.

He held her close. "Happy, Emma?"

"I think so. Yes. Happy and a little scared of what we're getting into."

"No need to be. We can handle whatever comes up."

She let the mischief shine in her eyes. "I can't wait till you get full use of your hand back."

He grinned. "Is sex going to be our main meeting point?"

"No doubt about it." She glanced at the leather sofa where they'd made such glorious love a few nights before. "And it won't always be in bed."

"I'd say you were a woman after my own heart, if you didn't already possess it," he ventured. "Although that's hardly sound medical thinking."

"You're not my doctor," she reminded him hoarsely.

"But I am your lover, and soon to be your husband. I don't want to wait too long for us to be together. "

"You don't have to. If my mother starts on about a lavish wedding, we'll threaten to elope." Lightness flooded her being, and a desire so strong she felt the floor shift under her feet. "Remember, she told me if I can't be a doctor, I might as well marry one."

His laughter made her toes curl. "And if I can't be a chef, I might as well marry one, too."

Having him put it that way touched her deeply. "I love you, Nate. I love how you see strengths in me I don't see in myself. How you appreciate my cooking..."

"Not to mention your sexy body," he cut in. "Do you really have to work today?"

About to remind him of tonight's commission, she made a decision. Start as you mean to go on. "Sophie can take it from here. I'm all yours."

As soon as the words left her mouth, Emma knew it was the truest thing she'd ever said.

\* \* \* \* \*

# COMING NEXT MONTH

### Available April 12, 2011

**#1698 RETURN TO THE BLACK HILLS**
*Spotlight on Sentinel Pass*
Debra Salonen

**#1699 THEN THERE WERE THREE**
*Count on a Cop*
Jeanie London

**#1700 A CHANCE IN THE NIGHT**
*Mama Jo's Boys*
Kimberly Van Meter

**#1701 A SCORE TO SETTLE**
*Project Justice*
Kara Lennox

**#1702 BURNING AMBITION**
*The Texas Firefighters*
Amy Knupp

**#1703 DESERVING OF LUKE**
*Going Back*
Tracy Wolff

HSRCNM0311

# REQUEST YOUR FREE BOOKS!
## 2 FREE NOVELS PLUS 2 FREE GIFTS!

**Harlequin**

*Super Romance*

### Exciting, emotional, unexpected!

HSR11

*Selene wanted nothing to do with the father of her son, Alex; but Aristedes had other plans...that included them.*

*Read on for an sneak peek from*
*THE SARANTOS SECRET BABY by Olivia Gates,*
*available April 2011, only from Harlequin Desire.*

"You were right to turn my marriage offer down," Aristedes said.

And Selene found her voice at last, found the words that would not betray the blow he'd dealt her. "Thanks for letting me know. You didn't have to come all the way here, though. You could have just let it go. I left yesterday with the understanding that this case is closed."

Before the hot needles behind her eyes could dissolve into an unforgivable display of stupidity and weakness, she began to close the door.

The door stopped against an immovable object. His flat palm.

"I can't accept that." His voice was low, leashed.

What did her tormentor mean now? Was he ending one game only to start another?

She raised eyes as bruised as her self-respect to his, found nothing there but solemnity and determination.

Before she could voice her confusion, he elaborated. "I never let anything go unless I'm certain it's unworkable. I realize I made you an unworkable offer, and that's why I'm withdrawing it. I'm here to offer something else. A workability study."

She leaned against the door, thankful for its support and partial shield. "Your son and I are not a business venture you can test for feasibility."

His gaze grew deeper, made her feel as if he was trying to delve into her mind, take control of it. "It's actually the other way around. I'm the one who would be tested."

She shook her head. "Why bother? I know—and *you* know—you're not workable. Not with me."

His spectacular eyebrows lowered over eyes she felt were emitting silver hypnosis. "You're right again. Neither you nor I have any reason to believe that isn't the truth. The only truth. It might be best for both you and Alex to never hear from me again, to forget I exist. But then again, maybe not. I'm only asking for the chance for both of us to find out for certain. You believe I'm unworkable in any personal relationship. I've lived my life based on that belief about myself. I never really had reason to question it. But I have one now. In fact, I have two."

*Find out what happens in*
*THE SARANTOS SECRET BABY by Olivia Gates,*
*available April 2011, only from Harlequin Desire.*

# SPECIAL EDITION

## Life, Love, Family and Top Authors!

In April, Harlequin Special Edition features
four *USA TODAY* bestselling authors!

### FORTUNE'S JUST DESSERTS
#### *by MARIE FERRARELLA*
Follow the latest drama featuring the ever-powerful
and passionate Fortune family.

### YOURS, MINE & OURS
#### *by JENNIFER GREEN*
Life can't get any more chaotic for Amanda Scott.
Divorced and a single mom, Amanda had given up on
the knight-in-shining-armor fairy tale until a friendship
with Mike becomes something a little more....

### THE BRIDE PLAN (*SECOND-CHANCE BRIDAL* MINISERIES)
#### *by KASEY MICHAELS*
Finding love and second chances for others is
second nature for bridal-shop owner Chessie.
But will *she* finally get her second chance?

### THE RANCHER'S DANCE
#### *by ALLISON LEIGH*
Return to the Double C Ranch this month—where love, loss
and new beginnings set the stage for Allison Leigh's latest title.

*Look for these titles and others in April 2011
from Harlequin Special Edition, wherever books are sold.*

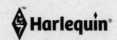

**Harlequin**®

A *Romance* FOR EVERY MOOD™

www.eHarlequin.com

# Harlequin Romance

# MARGARET WAY

## In the Australian Billionaire's Arms

Handsome billionaire David Wainwright isn't about to let his favorite uncle be taken for all he's worth by mysterious and undeniably attractive florist Sonya Erickson.

But David soon discovers that Sonya's no greedy gold digger. And as sparks sizzle between them, will the rugged Australian embrace the secrets of her past so they can have a chance at a future together?

*Don't miss this incredible new tale,*
*available in April 2011*
*wherever books are sold!*

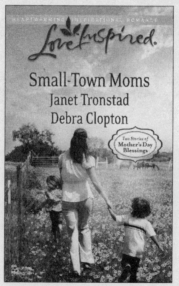